DHAMPIR,

THE BLOOD CURSE

ZOE JACKSON

The day was grey in all of its hurried shivers, as was the day before, and the day before that. It had always appeared that the western coast of New England was holding a funeral. But that was lost on Jared Jace, who was once again too concerned with the blueprints of his new project - constructing a multi-million dollar facility in the downtown area of West Haven, Maine.

He told himself that that was his primary concern. He was acting like it too; going about the day, as usual, stopping by Starbucks to pick up his caramel Frappuccino blend, dropping off his clothes at the cleaners, and picking up his prescriptions. Nothing unusual, yet, nothing was ordinary.

As he hurried home, tearing into the package that held one of the three vials of liquids that he had purchased, he prepared himself for the needle, tapping his arm to summon a vein. He injected the elixir, closing his eyes as the latest potion settled in his body, promising to sway the side effects of his curse. Damn the world, he thought. Damn it, for the world had damned him. He reclined back in his chair, refusing to move until his cell phone rang.

"Hello."

"Yo bro… did you do it?"

"Yeah, for what it's worth."

"Well?"

"Well, what… I just took it less than fifteen minutes ago. I can't see anything yet."

'Nothing?"

"Nothing… I'm going to give it a little more time. Call back in 30 minutes."

"What about the blueprints?"

"Look, Tyler… bro, it's been a rough day. I'm tired. I haven't had time to go over them."

"I'm not asking for me. Old man Watson wanted to know."

"Well, Watson has to wait."

"Okay, I'll let him know… look, man; you're not in this alone. We are in this together, remember? Always remember that."

"I know. It just seems that I'm alone."

"Our curses are the same, yet different. I have my cross to bear also, you know?"

"I know."

<silence 6 seconds>

"Ughhhhhh!"

"What's wrong?"

"Ugrrr… the medicine, it's starting to take effect."

"Jared… Jared, you want me to come over?!"

"No…ugh… yes. Yes, come over."

"Okay, I'm about 20 minutes away, should be there by seven."

"Okay, hurry!"

CLAYTON JACE WAS A HARD MAN, confident, determined, and cruel and ruthless, but he looked out for his boys. Yet inheriting a successful architectural firm didn't insulate Jared and Tyler Jace from the world's ills. Jace & Jace Architects was among the world's largest and successful architect companies, hiring over a thousand employees worldwide and earning over 567 million dollars annually. It took years for the company to bounce back from near ruins. After Clayton's mysterious death, both Jared and Tyler inherited 40 % of the company's stock, 18% going towards Wilbert Watson, Clayton Jace's closest friend, and business partner, and 2% divided amongst various minority investors. Although Jared was the younger of the two brothers, it was he who had become the face of the company – not that Tyler much cared. He was content with living a care-free lifestyle, albeit lavish, away from the spotlight. Even when he was required to attend board meetings, he never stayed to the end. It just wasn't his style, especially now, not since the curse.

No one paid attention to the bat crazy lady who waged a war of words on behalf of her jilted daughter. After all, she was one of the unfortunate ones, living modestly, on the wrong side of town. No one took her seriously when she accused one of West Haven's prominent sons of taking improprieties with her young daughter.

Her daughter, Jehona, was a second-generation Albanian, whose grandparents came to America, circa 1990, escaping the Bosnia / Serbia conflict. This place, with its sleepy town manners and cobblestone streets (especially downtown), reminded them of home before the war. It was here, in West Haven, that they decided to settle.

At the time, Clayton Jace was a bright young man, studying pre-law at the community college in 1993. There he met Jehona, all big brown-eyed with dark curly-haired, working in the school's library. Though not sophisticated in the ways of America, she was an intelligent girl with an illuminating smile. She was pretty, and Clayton took to her instantly. The two began attending public outings, despite the disapproval of both sets of parents.

But neither parents had to worry. It wasn't long before another captured Clayton's eyes. It happens all the time in the USA; boy meets girl, the two rendezvous, then go their separate ways. End of story. But when there are two different cultures involved, sometimes the ending just isn't so nip-tucked and neat. Sometimes payments are required. Sometimes retributions are demanded.

There were rumors that Jehona's parents had been

gypsies in their former land. Her parents, especially her mother, felt her daughter had been nothing more than a minor convenience for Clayton, a plaything to be used until he'd had his fill of her. No one was claiming rape, but her honor was at stake, and no one was there to uphold it. In her culture, the daughter's misfortune had cast shame on her family. Someone had to pay. There was only one way to quiet things over: Clayton Jace had to marry Jehona Bushati-Kartallozi.

Of course, this was deemed crazy in Clayton's world - undoubtedly laughable. Her family was now American citizens – no way would he subscribe to some antiquated, old fashioned custom. He hadn't broken any law. The girl was of legal age. They simply had sex, that was all, and both had consented. As far as Clayton was concerned, it was much ado about nothing. He decided to move on after filing a restraining order against the family, the mother in particular.

After eight months, Clayton ran into the mother at a local bakery. He wasn't sure it was her, viewing her from the side. But a closer look revealed the bitter scowled expression that he'd remembered. It was indeed her. He froze. He tried to utter a form of greeting, but could only come up with a shitty half-smile like women do when a strange man is approaching. At any rate, she said nothing, turned and got in line to pay for her items. Clayton remembered Jehona telling him that her mother kept her last name, but dropped her married name after her biological father died. Noticing she had a large basket of bakery goods, he offered to pay for them.

"I will be paying for Mrs. Bushati's order," Clayton said to the cashier, handing him his credit card. He was mildly surprised that Mrs. Bushati didn't intervene with the transaction. Maybe she had forgiven him, but she said nothing. After the purchase, she gathered her belongings and headed out the door.

"Wow, that was certainly strange. That lady didn't even bother to thank you," the cashier said, shaking his head. "How rude."

"Trust me, her not thanking me is the least of my worries, it could be worse. I'm just glad a gun wasn't around." The two men laughed.

When Clayton exited the store, Mrs. Bushati was on the sidewalk, waiting for him. She stared at him, nefariously without saying a word. In his awkwardness, Clayton felt compelled to say something, even though he wished he was 100 miles away from this crazy woman.

"How's the family... how's Jehona?" The words escaped his lips, nervously.

Still, not a word from Mrs. Bushati.

"Well... I guess I should be moving along, got a busy day ahead. It was nice seeing you."

It wasn't until Clayton had passed that Mrs. Bushati decided to address him, in her thick Albanian accent.

"You dare mention my Jehona... you Americans, with your busy days." She made an inaudible noise, said something in her native tongue, then spit on the ground, as if she was purging herself of a foul taste.

"You take and take and take. It's never enough!"

At first, Clayton didn't speak. He wouldn't dare. He knew the woman hated him, and quite frankly, he was afraid of her.

"It's because of you that my Jehona isn't here. Because of you!"

"Wha... where is Jehona? Is she okay?'

"As if you care... you care about no one."

"I do care, Mrs. Bushati. I cared for your daughter. I just wasn't ready to get married."

"If you cared, you would have married her. She was a good decent girl before you. I blame you, you hear me. You!"

"Mrs. Bushati, you keep referring to Jehona in the past tense. Did something happen to Jehona?"

Mrs. Bushati didn't answer. Instead, she rewrapped her head and face in the shawl that was resting on her shoulders. She gathered her groceries, then proceeded to walk past him. Only then did she speak. "This isn't over. It will never be over. You will suffer as you made me and my family suffer."

"What? Are you insane? I've done nothing to you. I think we should all reset and start –"

"Shut up! I curse you. I curse you, do you hear me?! Your future offsprings shall bear the mark of the blood curse. Your first-born will be half Lycan, a wolf beast!

While your second born will be stricken with the thirst for blood. You shall know what it is to suffer."

Clayton laughed. He couldn't believe he was in the middle of a horror script – a bad one at that. He was through with this hag. She had flipped her lid. He wouldn't bother to continue being polite to her.

"Okay, Mrs. Bushati. I'm gonna leave you to your own devices. You are delusional, crazy, but have it your way. I've gotta run," he said, trying to hold back his laughter.

"Begone, go!" she said with a wicked smile. "I'm finished with you."

"Good. Try to have a great day."

CHAPTER 2

"Take deep sips. That's it, that's it. Slowly," Tyler instructed his brother as he held a glass of warm tea to his mouth. "Are you in any pain?"

"A little, not like before," Jared groaned. "I hate this shit. I hate this. Why us, Tyler? Why in the world did this have to happen to us?"

"I don't know… I guess it's the sins of the father if you want to believe that, but then, I guess it's all in the way you look at things, accept things. Why, in all the world, are we so blessed to be filthy rich? Why us? See how things equal out? Not bad, huh?"

"Yeah, I guess… but do you believe it? Do you believe we are cursed?" Jared asked.

"Well, father believed it. He did a good job of convincing Watson, and so far, the evidence supports it. I have long accepted that we are different."

"But not so much you... you haven't experienced anything different."

Tyler looked at his hands and intertwined his fingers as if one was saying a prayer. There was something he hadn't told his brother.

"Jared, I haven't been open with you. I've had blackouts... waking up in strange places and not recalling how I got there."

"I know, you told me, you said you got stoned the night before. It happens."

"But, it happened again."

"It did? When?"

"Several days ago. I believe six, six days ago. I was afraid to mention it."

Jared didn't respond. He was busy looking something up on his notepad. "Let's see. I'm willing to bet your last blackout was five days ago."

"I don't know. Perhaps, why do you say that?"

"It says here, there was a full moon five days ago, March 12th."

Both brothers sat silently, coming to grasp with their fate. The truth shattered every strain of denial. This situation couldn't be real – not in 2019, the age of science and everything practical. But it is real, as real as cold concrete.

"So are we turning into monsters? Are we supposed to accept this? Right now, my stomach feels like it's turning inside out, this insatiable craving. Am I craving blood, Tyler?"

Tyler just sat and listened to his brother's questions - questions that he had no answers.

"And all this week, I wondered why I had headaches that I've never experienced before. I'm slowly, gradually becoming more and more sensitive to daylight. Fuck, fuck, fuck! What did father do?" Jared asked, looking up from where he was lying, the pain in his voice ever so evident, sniffing, on the verge of crying. "What could he have done that was so horrible to cause all of this?"

"Be strong, brother. Watson will know what to do. He will help us, and if not, we will help ourselves. Now is not the time for self-pity. We must first seek out the person responsible for this. Surely, she'll see what she has done. She'll want to reverse the curse."

"And what if she doesn't?"

"If she doesn't... then may God have mercy on her soul."

The next day at the office took a lot out of Jared. He had to reconstruct a building design before submitting it to a client. The client stubbornly wanted a linear settlement pattern (a pattern of buildings that are lined up and most likely found on steep hillsides) amid downtown, which went against every design in that particular area. Jared would have to convince the idiot to go with a dispersed settlement pattern, or at the very least, a nucleated settlement pattern (a design featuring buildings grouped that complemented the landscape better). The plan was to grow upwards, not out.

Like most of Maine's coastal cities, West Haven is laden in tradition. Early colonized farmers founded it, and every generation since has tried to preserve that heritage. There are artifacts of old oxen yokes, peaveys, stoves, plows, barrows, picaroons, saws, and chains can be found in several museums around the city, some dating back to 1825 - shortly after Maine joined the union.

Over the last 15 years, the city's Chamber of Commerce had gone all-out advertising West Haven's many natural and human-made attractions. It's the main reason Jace & Jace Architects was landing more than its share of the state's contracts, and if Jared had his way, the company would monopolize this state for years to come.

"You gonna eat that tuna sandwich, or what?" Jared inquired, pointing to the sandwich wrapped in parchment paper, over a pretty girl's shoulder.

"It depends… who wants to know?"

The inquisitive one was Nayla Lloyd, she of the timeless stance, elegant legs, and quick wit. She was fresh bait, having worked at Jace & Jace all of 6 weeks, and Jared had a thing for her.

"The man you're hopelessly in love with, but don't know it… yet."

"Hmmm, not yet, huh?"

"No, not yet. But you will."

"Oh, what makes you say that?"

"Because I have that way," Jared said, extending his neck and adjusting his collar.

Nayla smiled.

"So, are you gonna be busy later on, or are you gonna continue to blow me off?"

"Mr. Jace, I've told you, I don't date the boss."

"I'm not your boss. You have a supervisor, and again, the name's Jared."

"Which reminds me, Jared, I have to finish my submissions, or I won't have a job," Nayla said.

"Okay... but you didn't answer my question."

"I think I clearly answered your question... besides, you roll through once a week. I don't know you."

"Okay, but are you gonna answer my question?"

"I've answered you!"

"No," he said, pointing. "...the sandwich. Are you gonna eat the sandwich?"

"Oh, you lil' ass, I swear..." Nayla laughed, tossing the sandwich at him.

"Thanks, is he in?"

"Who, Mr. Watson? I think so. I can call him for you."

"Don't bother. Watson should be around the corner."

Few people knew that Wilbert Watson was actually in charge of the day to day operations at Jace & Jace Architects – not Jared, even though he was on the governing boards, and generally recognized as the CEO. The boys were only 16 and 17 when their father died, so it was no need to rush them into the business. Now at the grand old ages of 23 and 25, the transition could be made without any fanfare. Jared, however, was comfortable with things remaining as they were. He saw no need to change what had been a prosperous combination. And though ambitious, he could still be that without assuming all of the responsibilities.

"WW, WHAT'S UP?" Jared said, greeting Watson as he laid the blueprints on his desk. "The asshole won't buckle, even after my explanation."

"Sonnavubitch! Did you tell him that we're running over six months behind on a job that's due in two years?"

"Yes, of course, I mention it," Jared lied. "But he wasn't hearing me out... kept talking about a linear settlement design for a downtown area."

"What?! What is he - a fucking frontiersman?!"

Jared laughed.

"These government assholes know nothing 'bout designs. There's no wonder this city is laid out so backward. They commissioned us to do the buildings, yet they don't trust our expertise. Fuck 'em! Damn clueless pricks! Let 'em get someone else for the job – we don't need 'em."

"Yes, but I would hate to lose this account," Jared said. "If we can make this work, you know there are tons of projects that'll follow."

"Maybe so... what else is going on? Did your brother ever get that trailer hitch put on his truck? I'm gonna need it for next weekend, you know."

"No, I don't think so... well, Tyler's in his own little

world sometimes. He didn't mention it to me. Why can't you put it in your car?"

"Because I don't have a 4-wheel drive. Your brother has that, plus it's a Hemi. The lil' shit... probably don't want me driving it."

"Only you would think that, WW. He's been busy."

"Busy, my ass! The last time he was busy was when he was in high school, busy avoiding his homework."

"Yeah, you're probably right," Jared chuckled. "WW... remember you said that if we ever had a problem with anything, to come to you first?"

"Yes... and I meant it. You boys are like my family. What's up?"

"Well... I've been experiencing headaches of late because I'm becoming more sensitive to daylight."

Watson's face took on a severe countenance. He knew about the curse because Jared's father had convinced him to look after his boys if something should ever befall them. He made Watson believe it was real, and to take it seriously, no matter how ridiculous it sounded. Watson swore on their father's death bed that the boys would have no worries. Jared and Tyler would be the sons he never had.

"Do you think it has something to do with..."

"... the curse? Yes. I'm sure it does."

"But Jared, how can you be so sure?"

Jared reached in his pockets and showed him two of the three vials he had been taking. "This is the medication I've been taking – to no avail – the shit doesn't work. I have this insatiable urge to eat raw meat, raw flesh, but it hasn't happened yet."

Watson stood up and paced around his office, with an unlit cigar in his mouth. "So, it's true. I'd hoped for so long that your father was speaking out of his mind. Even when the years went by, and nothing happened, I was becoming convinced that the old boy had some type of cabin fever that had affected him, from all of those journeys he'd taken in South America and Europe, but it's true."

"Yes… I think so."

"So, how are you feeling now?"

"I'm holding on, but the urge is getting stronger."

"Have you been eating?"

"Yes… some, but I'm not satisfied. One other thing."

"What?"

"Tyler's been showing some signs also… he said he's been waking up places, but can't remember how he got there."

"Damn it! I told both of you to come to me first!" Watson sat back down and immediately started going through his roller deck.

"What are you doing?"

"Your father gave me a number seven years ago. I swore I would use it when this occasion came up. I didn't think I would ever need it. Hey, do me a favor, will you? Call your brother, get his butt in here, now!"

CHAPTER 3

Jared, Tyler, and Watson had dropped everything and were on a flight to Central Europe, per their father's instructions. From there, they were to meet a lady from Sarajevo, Bosnia, and Herzegovina. No one knew exactly the purpose of the mission, but they suspected that it might lead them to the answer for the curse. Before leaving, a female body had been found in the woods near West Haven Park. She had been mutilated and left partially clothed. The three dared not comment. No one knew. They just sat silently and tried to rest for most of the 15-hour journey.

When they arrived at Sarajevo Airport at 3:38 pm, Tyler and Watson were hungry, but not Jared. They rented a car and found a place to dine at a bistro terrace, facing a river next to a city park. The country was old and beautiful, featuring buildings from the 9th century, maybe earlier, which was part of the city's charm. The people, consisting mainly of Bosnians, Serbs, and Croats, were all friendly, though few spoke English.

"I have a question," Tyler said. "How long are we gonna be here?"

"Why… are you slated to be at a board meeting?" Watson said, hinting at his aversion to Tyler, missing so many board meetings.

"No… I just wanted to know."

"We are gonna be here for as long as it takes. I'm to follow these instructions upon arrival. My question for you guys is, since we all packed light, should I book a hotel now, or should I wait until after we meet with her?"

"I say book one now. I'm a little tired. A hot shower would do me good," Jared said.

"I think we should go ahead and get this over. We can be home by this time tomorrow," said Tyler.

"Well, I don't know. I kinda like this place, never been to this part of the world. It reminds me of a simple place in time. You kids should take time to appreciate the beauty."

"Yeah, Tyler," Jared said, flipping Tyler's baseball cap off his head. Appreciate the beauty, sucker.

"Let's just play it by ear. Let's call first, see how far we are from our destination, and get a hotel based on that, okay?" Watson said.

"Fine with me," said Jared. Tyler barely mumbled.

The trio followed the directions to 3 Stjepana Tomica

27, which from the onset, looked to be an old, dilapidated castle, resting on a high hill overlooking a river. It was small, by castle standard, but then, they had known very few castles to compare. When they pulled up in the circular driveway, a tall, stoic man, who smiled uneasily, greeted them.

"Hello, welcome to Castle Simijova Gruda," the man said in surprisingly good English. "My name is Mehmed. Lady Dautbegovic is expecting you."

"Hello Mehmed, I'm Wilbert Watson. My young associates here are Jared and Tyler Jace."

"A pleasure… please follow me."

Jared and Tyler looked at each other, holding back their laughter. Watson caught the notion and gave them a scornful look. "Something funny, guys?"

"No," they said in unison.

"You'd do well to take this seriously."

"Yessir."

The castle looked better on the inside. It was commodious, as one would imagine, with minimal furniture, and the furniture that was present looked antiquated and steeped in tradition. One could hear echoes in the hallowing chambers, which enhanced the eerie ambiance.

"I'm sorry, but this is too creepy," Jared found himself saying. Watson didn't try to silence him, because he was thinking the same thing. Mehmed led them to a separate chamber with better lighting, which enhanced everybody's mood. The furniture was noticeably more modern, too.

"May I get you some refreshments?" Mehmed said.

"Perhaps water – bottled water, if you have some… make it three," Watson said, speaking for Jared and Tyler.

"Of course. I'll be back. Please make yourself at home," Mehmed said.

"Thank you."

"That dude's creepy," Tyler said when Mehmed was out of sight. "Please, I dare someone try to deny that this isn't a scene from one of those old Boris Karloff movies, 'Dracula meets… whomever'," he laughed.

"Well, all I know is, I'm craving a hamburger, raw."

"You should have eaten back at the tavern."

"I wasn't hungry then. It's okay, I'll manage," said Jared. "Ahem…"

Mehmed had returned, accompanied by a thin elderly lady, adorned in a gross amount of jewelry. One could tell that at one time, she clung to her beauty like leaves in the springtime.

"Gentlemen, I present to you, Lady Jasmina Dautbegovic," he said, bowing, which was a signal for them to stand and stoop too. They took their seats only after Lady Dautbegovic was seated, across from them in a large chair.

"Gentlemen, I trust you had a pleasant flight," she said in a thick Bosnian accent, but otherwise perfect English.

"Yes, ma'am, we did. Lady Dautbegovic, I'm Wilbert Watson, and I would like for you to meet my associates, Jared and Tyler Jace."

Lady Dautbegovic looked at the young men without

actually acknowledging them. "Please, drop the formalities. You are amongst friends here, shall we get to the business at hand?"

"Ah, yes… as you know, I was given your number by the boy's father in case I needed to use it. Well, that time has arrived."

"I see," she said, and then took a sip of water from an ornate goblet. Only then did she specifically address Jared and Tyler. "I knew your father. He sought out my help over twenty years ago. I guess the information I gave him was of little use." She took another sip. "Mehmed, you may go."

"Yes, m' lady."

"I will tell you all that I know. Hopefully, you're not too late. The lady who placed this curse on you is my sister. How much do you know about your affliction?"

"Little of nothing," Tyler admitted.

"Your symptoms, what are they?"

"I've been waking up in places, but can't remember how I got there, I usually wake without my shirt and… I don't know, it just feels weird, like I've been fighting and running all night." Tyler said. "My brother has been having headaches and insatiable cravings for raw meat and blood."

"You are a Lycan, a werewolf," Lady Dautbegovic said, bluntly. "Your brother is exhibiting signs of vampirism – not yet fully blown, but it won't be too far."

"So, is there anything we can do about it?"

She stared at Jared and Tyler, looking into each of their

eyes. "Yes, stop pissing off evil, malicious women, like your father... but maybe I can give you some advice."

"What? Anything," Watson pleaded.

"The easiest way to get over your affliction is to go ask my sister to reverse the curse... but you'd have better luck putting out a fire in hell. She's a vindictive witch, been bitter and evil since she was a little girl, even more so since her daughter committed suicide."

"Wait, you said her daughter committed suicide?"

"Yes, some years ago."

"Was this the daughter that used to date the boys' father?" Watson asked.

"Yes, I thought you knew. It's why you're here, is it not? It's why the curse came about."

"I never knew... so that is what this is all about. I don't think Clayton knew the fate of the girl. I'm sure he didn't, he would've mentioned it."

"Well, if you ask me, I'm not so sure it was suicide. It was never proven, and if it was, my niece certainly wanted to get away from her mother desperately. She was desperate. In fact, she asked if she could move in with me. Her mother would've never gone for that, but I told her that she was welcome. She never called back. A month later, I heard she had died. That was around 1994."

"I'm sorry."

"Me too, she deserved better in life. She was a kind soul."

"Your sister... is she still alive?"

"Yes, but I haven't seen or spoken to her for over 30

years, ever since she drowned my cat, among other things. We would have long destroyed one another."

"So, you're telling me there's no other way, no hope for them," Watson asked.

"No, I'm not. There might be another way, but it's a long shot, it won't be easy. The best way to defeat or overcome anything is first to know exactly who or what you're dealing with, wouldn't you agree?"

"Yes, of course."

"I'm going to tell you a tale," Lady Dautbegovic said, sipping from her goblet. "Maybe this will give you a better grasp of the task that lies before you. You need to know as I know, see as I see, feel as I feel, know that eons ago, before Stonehenge, before Easter Island and the Great Pyramids of Egypt, seemingly before time itself when the world was young, a blood pact was made in a Neolithic era. Their names are not essential, but I'll tell you anyway. They were Ira, Abigail and Elex, three friends.

The friends had made many pacts during their gatherings in their secret cave, but this one was different. Each cut their hand and watched the crimson substance flow into a wooden bowl, over various herbs and the heart of a waterfowl. After declaring the pact was sealed and couldn't be aborted until the same blood was spilled, Abigail held up a crystal that was worn around her neck, sealing the agreement.

"Zoaban maaymon marrach hiiatratu ubatus... Zoaban maaymon marrach hiiatratu ubatus," they chanted, unbeknownst that a spirit resided in the cave. A force neither understood nor had ever experienced knocked them off their feet, hurling them to different sides of the cave. Gathering themselves, confused but otherwise unharmed, the three friends dusted themselves off and began to hover around the blood-covered crystal.

"Wha.. what was that?"

"Only the Mother Goddess knows for sure," Elex said, watching the glow wane until it eventually stopped. The crystal suddenly absorbed the blood that had been spilled on it as if it was a sponge. Amazed, the three looked in horror at each other and concluded that it was a sign from the gods, and must be our secret.

Now please remember, this was an era before science. When something defied logic, it was attributed to being a sign from the gods," Lady Dautbegovic said, interrupting her story.

"That's understandable. The people of that time weren't as enlightened or as smart as we are today," said Watson, rolling his eyes.

That brought a smile to Lady Dautbegovic, and then she paused for a sip of water.

"In all fairness to them, that would be hard to explain even with today's technology," Jared sharply noted.

"That's correct, young man. Okay, so, where was I?"

"You were talking about the crystal… how it absorbed the blood."

"Oh yes," she said, continuing.

" So after that episode with the blood being absorbed on the amulet, Abigail reluctantly placed it back around her neck, and the friends felt it was time to go home, but not before swearing again to uphold their secret. "We tell no one, not even our parents or the High Priestess," they swore.

Abigail Stewardson's family consisted of Druids and Wiccans (we call them witches today). They believed in a spiritual, harmonious way of life and advocated against human sacrifices, which didn't always align with the village's customs, the Orcladics. With that said, Abigail's family were the most potent wielders in the land, meaning their innate psychokinetic powers enabled them to see into the future and cast spells. Her parents held a firm position within the village. They were in tune with the forces of nature and had a profound knowledge of herbs and medicines, which naturally made them the village healers. They were well-loved and respected and fought for righteousness for the less fortunate. However, their position threatened the authority of the High Priestess, who was well-grounded in paganism. It was only because of their healing expertise that no sacrificial attempts ever made on their lives.

As one might suspect, the Stewardsons were proud people, and grateful for their position within the village. Still, no one understood the true nature of Abigail's powers, not even Abigail herself. Though all in her family were seers, she was bestowed with the unique gift of being a 10th generational wielder, and this was important because only one person was elected to learn how to hone and master the gift. With being the 10th, the powers of the previous nine generations were bequeathed upon her. Thus was the oracle, the path chosen by their ancestors to help strengthen their abilities and keep the Dark Ones, as they were known, at bay.

The Orcladics' primary purpose was to ensure their village protection against their enemies and to find a successor to their Elder. On the other hand, the Dark Ones wanted nothing more than the destruction of the Orcladics, the Stewardsons bloodline in particular. Led by their leader, Asyla Maluco, the Dark Ones were feared because of their savagery and barbaric customs. Unlike the Orcladics, who was slowly rounding out of the Mesolithic period and advocated a peaceful existence, the Dark Ones were slaves to their primal instincts, giving way to violence, human sacrifices, and pillaging.

Of course, none promoted this more than Asyla. Blessed with ravishing beauty and cunning wiles, she would be considered a psychopath and insane by today's standards. Yet, she was a skilled craftsman, a deft practitioner of the dark arts in her own right, and had no issue using her craft against her people whenever her servants couldn't capture a neighboring villager.

"Damn, Asyla was the Big Kahuna back in her day," Tyler said.

"Yes, I would say so, if ruling by fear is your thing," Watson retorted. "So. my question is… well, I'm getting a sense there's gonna be this big showdown between Abigail and the other girl, ahh…"

"Asyla."

"Yeah, Asyla. My question is, who whipped whose ass, and why did Asyla have beef with Abigail? I mean, they never met, did they?"

"I don't know. I would suspect that Asyla was acutely aware of Abigail, perhaps through word of mouth, who knows? Asyla was obsessed with the Stewardsons' destruction because she felt they were the only thing that stood in her way, thus preventing her from amassing omnipotent power over the clans and ruling supreme. Her every waking hour centered around upending them."

"Was Asyla as powerful as Abigail?"

"Aaah, you're getting to the crux of my story, young man," Lady Dautbegovic said, seeming to take delight in Jared's interest. "She had similar powers but derived them differently. Remember, when I told you how Abigail gained her strength?"

"Yes… by being a tenth generational weider, correct?"

"Right, just checking to see if you were paying attention," Lady Dautbegovic sniggered. "Well, Asyla, gained her powers primarily through ritual sacrifices. By using the hair of a seduced Stewardsons' kin and her blood, she was able to invoke a spell that gained strength through time by summoning the archaic spirit of Nyi'el, the god of the night.

Because the Dark Ones thought little of people without wealth or influence, there was no limit to how many people Asyla slaughtered. Many were due to sacrificial offerings to Nyi'el. Still, more can be credited to her own savage bloodlust. She had stolen years from her clan by consuming their blood, thereby retaining her youth, beauty, and vitality.

Asyla ruled for decades before her people started noticing she wasn't aging. Strife and bitter dissension began to settle in amongst her village. When a young child's body showed up, void of blood and dumped in a moss bog near her lair, they knew she was the culprit. The clan turned on her, but before she could be brought to justice and pay for her transgressions, she escaped to a secret cave along with three servants and conjured up a spell of immortality."

"Immortality?"

"Yes, immortality."

"Damn, so that means she can't die."

"It means she can't die of natural causes, but she can be destroyed."

"Wow, cool!" Jared uttered.

Lady Dautbegovic continued. "The spell insured three things. Asyla would obtain immortality, but she would be subjected to long periods of rest. Secondly, while awake, she would require blood to sustain her, and last, her victims would also assume immortality, and the afflicted could pass on the inherited genetic code of their "mother," Asyla. Thus, you have the vampire curse, gentlemen."

"Wow, kinda like in the movies, evil versus good," Jared said.

"Yes, but who is which? I guess it all depends on one's perspective," said Tyler.

"The story of the vampire and the werewolf has been severely watered down through the ages. We marvel at Hollywood, the way they enhance a story to sell tickets, regardless of reaching out for facts."

"Which are?"

"They are not as clandestine as we would like to think... vampires and werewolves walk among us. Most have mastered the illusion of modern living; they blend in and do whatever's necessary to survive without calling attention to themselves. Immortality has served them well."

"So, you're saying there are others like my brother and me?" Tyler asked.

"Oh, god, yes! Many. I've spoken to several myself, sitting in the exact chair you're sitting."

"That's fantastic, simply amazing.

"It's the truth, but getting back to my story... there were many altercations between the two tribes, but generally they tried to avoid the other. It didn't deter Asyla's relentless attacks on Abigail, however. She conquered spell after spell, trying to come up with the right curse to weaken and defeat Abigail. Through it all, Abigail never suffered any ill effects from Asyla's curses because her family's spells protected her. The same could not be said for her friends. While during a physical conflict with Asyla's clan, Elex suffered a wound from one of her minions, and Ira befriended a dire wolf. He was bitten accidentally during a hunting expedition, according to *The Rodolmen*. The circumstances behind their affliction weren't proven to be witchcraft, but then, who would've known? It's documented that the two were never the same, and behaved 'inhuman'... there was minimal mention of them after that."

"Waitaminute, go back. You said it's documented in the what?" asked Tyler.

"*The Rodolmen*... it's kind of like a Hungarian bible, meaning 'bloodline'," Lady Dautbegovic said.

"So, all of this is documented somewhere?"

"Absolutely... why else would I know and be telling you about it?" Lady Dautbegovic paused, seemingly for dramatic effect and sipped again of her water, standing. "You may follow me," she said. Lady Dautbegovic then walked to a glass-encased stand. The soft light illuminated the stand where a single book laid open. "This is The Rodolmen, been passed down for centuries," Lady Dautbegovic said of the old tattered book, written in ancient Hungarian. "So, should I go on?"

"Yes, we're all ears, believe me," Watson said, speaking for everyone, now with heightened anticipation.

"Anyway, as the legend goes, Asyla wasn't successful in defeating the Stewardsons clan – not in her time. They were simply too powerful. But she was effective in imposing her influence and creating a chain of events that has affected civilization to this day. Using her craft and employing yet another spell, she and three of her most trusted servants went into a self-imposed slumber, so deep that it was considered an eternal sleep. The spell would awaken her servants ten days before her inevitable awakening, to prepare for her arrival. By you being here, it's obvious that time is upon us."

"Miss Dautbegovic… I mean, Lady Dautbegovic, you said there was a way to reverse all of this."

"I said there 'might' be a way."

"Which is?"

"Well. If you believe *The Rodolmen,* which I do, it tells of seven awakenings over five periods in time. We are all aware that Asyla has been awakened before, sometime back in the 14th century, during the time of the Black Death in Europe, she walked the earth. It was the first time chronicled; the last time was in the early 20th century, during the Russian Civil War in 1921, each time stronger than before. If you notice, the intervals between her sleep are getting shorter and shorter.

"Yes.., I've noticed," Watson said. 'Why is that?"

"Because she's getting stronger, her powers have grown after being invoked after ten generations. I'm sure she has survived 70 or 80 generations since. What's time to her? And she always appears when humanity is experiencing woe and hardships during wars, plagues, and natural disasters. Why do you think that is?"

"… because she's feasting, she can blend in without being noticed?"

"Yes. It's very true. The best tool that the demon has for survival is anonymity. Who's going to notice a few hundred people missing during a war? Chaos is its best friend because it doesn't like to call attention to itself. We have cast aspersions, stigmatized, defiled, and vilified a creature for doing something that comes naturally to us all – and that is to feed and survive," Lady Dautbegovic said, seemingly sympathizing with the creature. "Yet we know that Asyla's only weakness is when she sleeps. It's when she's most vulnerable – she can be defeated, but she needs The Sacred Amulet of Abigail to free herself of being only a creature of the night. If she obtains it, her powers will have no limitation - only a spell by a creature just as powerful as she could stop her, but there is hope. Remember me telling you that there were seven awakenings?"

"Yes, of course."

"Four are Asyla and her three servants. The other three awakenings are believed to be Abigail, Ira, and Elex."

"So you said 'believed to be', meaning you don't know for sure?"

"No, because parts of the documents are faded away. You have to understand; the Rodolmen is very ancient. Something that old is subjected to a lot of wear and tear, even under the most favorable conditions."

"Understandable."

"It is believed that Asyla's awakening happens five days before Abigail's, which gives her a five-day head start to search for the crystal amulet. Abigail had opposed her in battle before and defeated her, probably doing a biblical period, but as I've mentioned, a large section of the book has faded away. I also can't tell you the role that Elex and Ira play. That part was damaged the most."

"So, we've heard the history of Asyla... she's supposed to be the first vampire or something, right?" Asked Tyler.

"Yes, a vampire-like creature. I wouldn't call her a vampire exactly, but she had a lot of vampirish similarities, yes." Lady Dautbegovic patiently answered.

"... and the werewolf?"

"Ira is presumed to be the first elder werewolf?"

"Interesting, very interesting. But what I need to know is, what all of us need to know is, how does that help us?" Jared said.

"To be honest, I can't say... I know what I know from The Rodolmen. What I can tell you is, you will know what to do before I know. You and your brother share a special kinship with Asyla, possibly with Abigail too. You'll sense it all around you, your sense of smell, sight, and heartbeat... you'll just know, even if you're half a world away. No other human being can be in tune with that. Look for the signs."

Watson reclined in his chair after hearing the incredible story, not sure whether or not he had just fallen prey to Bosnian folklore. "Amazing... amazing!" He found himself uttering. Jared and Tyler paused as if they had just suddenly started to listen to her, but in reality, they had been listening all along. It was just that now it seemed more real, with Lady Dautbegovic sitting right before them, with documentation in The Rodolmen, and the legend itself. No matter how much they wanted to dismiss it as a fairytale, they knew it was all too real.

"It's hard to believe," said Jared. "You appear to know a lot about the history… just wondering, why did you take an interest?"

Lady Dautbegovic once again sipped from her goblet. "That's an easy one for me to answer, young man. I was surprised you didn't ask me how I had come about ownership of The Rodolmen. You see, my bloodline's linked to Asyla Maluco, I'm a direct descendent."

Watson and the young men grasped.

CHAPTER 4

March 27, 2017, almost two weeks since their trip to Europe, few things had changed. Jared decided to move in with Tyler because they both agreed it would be a better-suited atmosphere in dealing with the new, expected developments in their lives. Tyler certainly had space. He lived in a capacious 2100 square foot, two-story house that was barely furnished, certainly more privacy than what Jared's swanky uptown condominium could provide. Both agreed that it would be a temporary arrangement, pending their circumstances, but they needed one another for the time being.

"Hey, bro, remember me telling you about the girl at work?" Jared said while sitting on a barstool, eating an apple. Tyler looked at him with a befuddled expression written across his face.

"You know, the one with the great ass and legs… Nayla, Nayla Lloyd."

"Oh yeahhh," Tyler said, feigning acknowledgment. The truth was that Jared, not unlike himself, always talked about girls with great tits and asses. He didn't remember which one he was referring.

"Well, she finally buckled… having her over tomorrow night. Dim the lights in the champagne room, hahaha! You gonna be home?"

"Tomorrow night? Naaah, having dinner with a special someone tomorrow, at her place."

"Aha! You ole sly fox, you."

"More like a sly wolf, wouldn't you say?" Tyler joked. The only thing, it wasn't funny, and Jared didn't laugh.

"When's the next phase?"

Tyler showed him a calendar with dates circled on it. "Tuesday, April 11th… how are you managing?"

"You don't want to know, trust me… it's disgusting."

"You're not hurting anybody, are you?!" Tyler asked in horror.

"Naaw bro, relax… been buying cattle and pig blood from slaughterhouses. They sell me quarts of the stuff without asking questions. Of course, I had it sterilized first, but it seems to work. I no longer have the cramping."

"Good," Tyler said. "Good… we're gonna make it through this. I just know we will. Come here, wanna show you something."

Jared followed Tyler downstairs to his basement.

There, he showed him a 20x15 cage he had built. "There… this baby is for me!" He said proudly. If I'm having episodes, if I'm changing, I want it to be witnessed and videoed by you."

"Okay," Jared said uneasily. He swallowed hard and said, "what if the cage doesn't hold you… what if you break out?"

"Are you kidding? Look at this! Look at it! It's the same thickness and strength that they use for building jail cells. Ain't nothing breaking out of this, would you like for me to shackle my ankles? Maybe my fuckin' neck?!" Tyler asked angrily.

Jared stared at Tyler without responding. "I'm sorry, bro… it's just that this whole situation is getting to me. I'm constantly reminded that I have to take precautions for everything because I might transform into a vicious, brutish animal."

"It's okay… remember, we're in this together, sink or swim," Jared said.

Tyler held him firmly by the shoulder, patting it. "It's gonna be okay… it's gotta be."

It was nearing 8:00 pm when Jared put the finishing touches on the meal he had brought to the house. He didn't cook it, he couldn't cook, but it was the most exquisite catered food that money could buy. On the menu was Pan-fried Scottish Scallops & Shrimp, with crispy capers, béarnaise sauce, and tendril pea shoots. For dessert, a Very Berry Cheesecake - simple but very tasty. His beverage of choice was a 2009 Classic Clare Riesling, white wine.

"There," he said, thinking out loud. "Perfect for an evening of seduction and debauchery."

Now, he would take a quick shower, and Nayla should be here shortly. It was all so perfect.

At 8:11 pm, the doorbell rang. It was Nayla Lloyd, of course. Who else could it be?

When Jared opened the door, Nayla was standing, all pretty, holding up a bottle of her own wine.

"Hey, Cutie… awww, that wasn't necessary. I already took care of the wine. Hmmm, let's see what you got. A Verada Pinot Noir, very good, perfect," he said while kissing her on the cheeks. "Did you have any problem finding the place?"

"No, not at all," she said, looking around the house. "Nice place. Big, lots of room…"

"And virtually void of furniture, yes, I know… it's actually my brother's place. I'm having renovations done at my place, so I'll be here for a while until the contractors are finished," Jared lied.

"You rich people are always having renovations and makeovers done to your homes… just have to find ways to spend all that money, huh?"

"Heeey, gotta keep it fresh, baby! Gotta keep it fresh, and speaking of fresh; you smell like a fresh bouquet."

"Thank you… I guess it beats the alternative."

"What's that?"

"Stinking… reeking like that man who came by the office yesterday."

"Hahahaha… I don't remember that, was I there?"

"No. Trust me, you wouldn't have wanted to smell that guy. I couldn't concentrate on my job after that. It was very distracting. God."

"Well, here, feast your eyes on this. Tell me what it smells like," Jared said, leading her to the table he had set up. He opened a shiny dome tray and let the aroma escape to her nostrils.

"Voila! I bet this smells better than your friend yesterday."

"Oh my God… did you cook this? It smells divine, and looks great!"

"I'm not saying I did. I'm not saying I didn't, but I suggest we dig in. What do you say?"

"You don't have to twist my arm. I'm hungry."

"Good."

The dinner was a huge success, and the wine was exquisite. The couple spent the evening relaxing, laughing, and getting to know each other. Jared could imagine spending more time with her, but it was her call.

"You know, I didn't like you when we first met," she admitted. "… thought you were the typical spoil, smug, egotistical rich boy.

"So what changed your mind, I might very well be as you thought."

"Nah, you're not. You're too kind, thoughtful, and gentle, and sweet, and, and," she said while closing her eyes to lie upon Jared's chest. Jared kissed her softly as if it was the first and only kiss he'd ever had. Her lips tasted of jasmine and a tinge of tangerine, her neck like soft velvet. He wanted more of her.

He led her by the hand to his bedroom, his room, dark, except for a lone red candle, flickering unchoreographed. A king-sized bed, minus the headboard, was the only furniture in the center of the spacious room. A single picture adorned the walls as a jazzy bossa nova tune played softly throughout the house. The evening was easy. It was right. They made love in that room until the rapid-fire on the lone red candle ceased to burn.

IT WAS 9:37 A.M., and Nayla was still sound asleep in the same position as the night before. Jared got up without awakening her and proceeded to wash up and go about his morning activities. It brought a smile to his face that Nayla was so comfortable in a stranger's bed. Maybe she simply couldn't handle the wine. At any rate, he wished that more girls were like her. He could tell by the keys on the living room table that Tyler had made it in from his date last night. He decided to check in on him while making coffee.

He peeped in and saw that Tyler was lying across his bed with his clothes still on. "Hey, bro, you're awake?"

Tyler made an inaudible noise. He needed more rest, so he left him alone. Jared would never be mistaken for a chef, but his toast and eggs were adequate. Nayla and himself. He was proud of the breakfast he had made, and couldn't wait to present it to Nayla. He poured a glass of orange juice, added a cup of cream and sugar for her coffee, laid a single red rose on her tray and presented it before her, as well as any waiter or concierge would have.

"Wake up, sleepyhead... breakfast is served."

Nayla didn't respond. He thought about letting her sleep more, but he wanted her to see the breakfast he'd prepared, so he tried waking her again.

"Nayla... Nayla baby, time to get up. Look what I have for you."

After she didn't respond for a second time, he pulled and turned her over by the shoulder, but was greeted by lifeless eyes, open, and staring at nothing. Startled, he dropped the tray on the bed and backed away from her.

"Nayla!" He cried and began shaking her. As her hair moved, he saw two puncture wounds on her neck and a trail of dried blood.

"Oh God... oh God... please... please no, this can't be happening... this can't be happening..."

He then stumbled into his brother's room, completely in a state of shock. At first, he just stood motionless, then called out.

"Tyler, wake up... Tyler, Tyler!"

"Wha... what is it? Why are you bothering me?!"

"She's dead."

"Wha… what?"

"She's dead… I… I… she's dead."

Tyler sat up from his bed, fully awake, and fearing the worst. "Jared, who's dead?"

"She's… she's…" He said, pointing, seemingly in a stupor.

Tyler raced upstairs into Tyler's bedroom. He saw the lifeless girl lying in bed, partially nude. "God, what have you done? Jared, what have you done?!" He shouted, at first angrily, then with compassion.

"I don't even remember it happening… I can't. I don't remember it…" Jared said, still in shock.

"Okay… Okay, just sit down. We're gonna figure this out." He gave Jared what was left of the orange juice he'd spilled. "Drink… try to remember. You bit her; marks are on her neck."

"I do not deny that I bit her, but I don't remember it… believe me. I don't remember, I don't want to go to jail," Jared said as he broke down.

"You're not going to jail… did anyone know the girl was coming to meet you last night?"

Jared didn't reply. He was still sobbing.

"Jared, fuckin' pull it together, man the fuck up! Now answer my question, did anybody –"

"No… I mean, Nayla lived alone. Nobody was around when I asked her to come over."

"You'd better hope not, for your sake… look, help me carry her down to the basement. We've got to get rid of the body sometime today. Hey, isn't she supposed to turn into a vampire after she dies or something?"

"I dunno… it's my first time being a vampire," Jared joked. I think that happens only in the movies, bro."

"Well, help me figure out where we're going to dispose of the body… we have to do it later tonight."

"Should we tell Watson?"

"You think he should know?"

"No… I don't want Watson to know. He's got enough on his plate, with the firm's projects. I just don't want him knowing if he doesn't have to know," Jared said.

"Okay, he doesn't have to know."

"Tyler… Thanks, bro. I mean, really, thanks."

"No problem… you'll do it for me."

After cleaning Nayla's body to the best of their abilities, and using gloves while handling her, Jared and Tyler decided to wrap the body in a plastic tarp sheathing that Tyler had lying around the house for constructing his cell. They then drove two counties away, and dumped the body underneath an uneven tarmac, on a run-down, dilapidated farm. The area was rural and free of all traffic. It looked untouched for years.

"I can't imagine anyone stumbling upon her body for months, maybe years… the longer she stays missing, the better for all of us, trust me."

Jared said nothing, for five miles, then he suddenly spoke. "I'm feeling nauseated. I think I'm going to puke."

Tyler stared at him, trying to determine if he was joking. "Are you for real, bro?"

"I'm hella real."

"Wait… I'll pull over!"

Jared tried to contain the vomit, getting some on the passenger's door, as he swung the door open. "Arggggggg… ahhhhhhh…" he grasped.

Tyler laughed. "Dude, we sure aren't cut out to be gangsters or bad boys. There's nothing hard about us, nothing."

"I know, right," Jared said, wiping his mouth. "But I'm glad I'm the way I am. I hope I never get used to this. I hope that I always regard human life as the most sacred thing on this planet. The girl, Nayla, was a good girl from a decent family. I hate that her family won't be able to give her a proper burial. I hate what I've become. I hate that I've become a monster, a scourge on God's green earth," he said, a lone tear running down his face.

"Jared, don't… we didn't ask for this – any of this. We just gotta do the best we can with the cards dealt. I mean, what else is there, besides killing ourselves."

Jared stared at Tyler, as though it was something he would seriously contemplate. But neither brother had the type of courage it would take to destroy themselves, so the thought was quickly dismissed.

"Do you wanna go to 'Godfrey's' for a drink… it'll be on me," Tyler said.

"Yes… yes, brother. I would. I could use a strong 'Long Island Iced Tea'."

"I like their 'Blue Lagoons'- ever had one?"

"Can't say I have... but I'm sticking with a 'tried & true', something I know I like, and I know it will give me a buzz."

"I'm feeling you."

WHAT A DIFFERENCE A DAY MAKES \ twenty-four different hours. Truer words had never been spoken, for Jared was feeling like a new man. No longer weighed by guilt and sorrow, he felt a measure of respite from having to deal with his inconceivable life. Five 'Long Island Iced Teas' has that effect.

He dropped by the office to see if Watson had made any progress on several of the new projects. He couldn't help but notice the vacant office cubicle that Nayla once occupied. On her desk was a picture of her and her mother, hugging and smiling, apparently attending her graduation ceremony. She was truly loved and nurtured, nourished by nature and ebullience. He left a single rose on her desk, looked straight ahead and pressed on.

CHAPTER 5

"Great news... here, take a look at this," Watson said, handing Jared a pile of blueprints. "Out of the 41 projects on the board, 37 are approved. Thirty-seven! That's what? 80, almost 90 percent! We haven't had that high of a percentage in three years! I'm telling you son, that Proposition 7 is freeing up a lot of money, which means more money for us."

"Damn WW, that's great... I guess this is cause for a celebration."

Watson thought for a minute and said, "Dammit, I can't see why the hell not!"

He poured both he and Jared a glass of cognac from his private stock on his portable bar.

"A toast. May good fortunes follow us all the days of our lives and, may we forever reap from the many restorations of the divine goblet of wealth."

Jared looked at him sideways, "Okayyy, I'll toast to that, I think."

"Don't worry. It's all good. And the best news of all is, I got those government bastards to go alone with the landscape proposal."

"You mean the one I've been working on?!"

"One and the very same."

"How did that happen?"

"You young cats don't realize all the tools you have ready at your disposal - you're still learning. Ever heard of the game of golf? You'd be surprised how many deals are made on the golf course. You should pick up the game."

"Why you old weasel. You should've been a pimp."

"Who said I'm not? It ain't easy, but somebody's gotta do it." The two men laughed.

BY THE END of the second drink, Jared decided to slow down. "I'm gonna have to call a truce," he said. "Tyler and I took on a round or two last night. I can't allow this kind of thing to become a habit."

"Ahhh, drink up. You'll be just fine. It'll put some bass in your voice."

"No, I shouldn't... got some more things I have to attend to, I need to keep a level head."

"Well, alright. I'll never force a man to drink my finest cognac," Watson smiled as he poured himself another round. "So, how's it going, living with Tyler?"

"Not bad, not bad at all. It's a big place. We barely see

each other. I guess we've finally grown up, since being young boys. We can now tolerate one another."

"Good, so what's going on with you - anything new?"

"Naah, same old, same old."

"So... no problems?"

"No, we haven't become monsters yet, if that's what you are trying to ask."

Watson sat on the corner of his desk, holding his cognac. He could sense Jared was becoming perturbed. God knows he had every right to be. The young man was dealt a bad hand. He could relate.

"You know, when I was a younger man, about your age, no... actually, I was younger, I almost dropped out of college. I mean, I didn't want to drop out, but I simply didn't have the finances, and couldn't figure out where I was going to get them. Now I know that my means for making anything out of my life rested on me getting an education, but what do you do when your family didn't have money? Luckily, I had met someone, and I guess I'd made an impression on them – hell, I don't know, I couldn't tell you – but have you ever met someone that genuinely likes you and you don't know why?"

"Yes... I guess."

"I mean, the person paid for my meals, would give me money for dates, sometimes paid for my transportation – the person carried me. I guess they felt sorry for me. They handed me an olive branch, even paid for my last year's college tuition."

"So, are you telling me you were a gigolo, WW?"

Watson chuckled. "No, noooo, far from that. I was a nerdy kid - wasn't remotely athletic or handsome – like I am today," he laughed. "I'm telling you this because my friend was your father. He handed me the olive branch, and saved my life, both figuratively and literally. I wouldn't be where I am today if it wasn't for him. I want you to know, as I've said countless times. If you guys need anything - ANYTHING – don't hesitate to let me know. I owe it to you."

"Appreciate it, WW, but all we need is for this damned curse to be lifted. Have you heard anything from that lady?"

"You mean, Lady Dautbegovic?"

"Yes"

"No, I doubt that I will. I think she told us everything she knows. Why, have you been noticing anything different? Remember, she said to look for the signs."

"Yes, but what signs? I haven't seen anything different. Neither have Tyler. Did you believe all that hocus pocus? I mean, some of it might make sense. But do you believe that mess about the vampire lady coming back to life? That's too far-fetched for me. I mean, really?"

"Well, it's a lot to have to swallow, but I believe in reincarnations... I believe in things that can never be explained through science. I believe in things I don't fully understand. So yes, I believe in curses," Watson said, driving home his point.

"Yeah... I see what you mean."

Later that night, Jared ate supper with Tyler. It was a take-out from an Italian restaurant. It was a chance for the brothers to go over and implement any plan they may need to devise.

"Saw Watson today."

"Oh yeah, what is he talking about, the old goat?"

"Not much. He was happy about securing most of the contracts we had on the board. I felt bad for him, though."

"Why?"

"Well, I kinda suggested that we celebrate, but I left him drinking alone," Jared said.

"That shouldn't have been a problem for Watson."

"It wasn't. Still, I wouldn't have liked drinking alone, in the middle of the day, especially when I..." Jared noticed that Tyler wasn't paying attention. He was there, but his mind was miles away. "Tyler?"

"Hey...ah, yeah, sorry."

"What's on your mind, what are you thinking about?"

"Was just thinking, in two days, there's a full moon."

"I know. I know, April 11th," Jared said. "What if it's not what you think? What if you're just simply paranoid? I mean, nothing's been proven. No one has ever seen you – even you can't remember."

"I can feel it. I just know something weird is going on with me. How can anyone explain my blackout episodes? You know, I wasn't going to say anything, but remember just before we left to go to Europe?"

"Yes."

"… remember, they'd found a girl murdered… mutilated?"

Jared sat quietly without answering while Tyler continued.

"I think… I think…"

"You didn't do it," Jared said.

"How can you say that? How do you know?"

"Because it happened three days after the full moon. I was curious, so I read up on it. It happened on the 15th of last month, so it couldn't have been you."

Tyler put his arm around his brother's shoulder. "I've got much love for you, lil' bro, much love. And I appreciate what you are trying to do, but they found the girl's body on February 15th. She was slain three or four days prior. So you see, it doesn't exclude me. Judging by the condition of the body, I'm more than likely responsible."

"The news said a bear mauled her."

"Of course they did. What else are they going to say? How many bear killings have we had in Maine? We have black bears here, but they seldom attack humans. It seldom if ever happens."

"Okay, if you want me to believe that you are a killer, okay. I give up," Jared said, holding up his hands.

"Jared, I don't like it. I hate it. But we have to accept what we are. Only then will we be able to take the necessary precautions in protecting ourselves and others. In two days, I will lock myself up. Then we will both know because you will be there too."

Saturday, March 11th came soon enough. It was 5:34 p.m., and Jared found himself more anxious than Tyler. Tyler was reclined on a chair in his sunroom, listening to a hip hop tune. The day had settled into a lazy gray haze, and the fog hung thick like an interim cloud. It was the kind of day that beckoned for a precise course. Jared could relate.

"When are you going in?" Jared asked while pulling up a chair, a foot away.

"Oh, I imagine an hour from now, maybe two."

"Are you scared?"

"No... remember, I'm the boogie man. Why am I afraid? Are you scared?"

"A little, I guess. I don't know what to expect."

Tyler looked at him. "You know exactly what to expect," he said. "We both do... look, if you're too scared to come down with me, at least turn on the camera and lock me in the basement."

"No, I want to come down there with you. That's the plan, right? I plan to be there for you."

"Thanks, this means a lot to me - a lot."

"It means a lot to me too."

"So, do you want to go down by seven?"

"Seven is as good a time as any."

Armed with two muffuletta sandwiches, two raw roast beef sandwiches (for Jared), chips & dip, a gallon of water, and a gallon of lemonade, the brothers descended to the basement. Jared also brought down a small television and a bag of cookies. This would not be spiritual fasting or any sort of sacrificial endeavor whatsoever the brothers joked. They would feast, and feast hardily.

"Ice, we forgot ice," Tyler said.

"We won't need it. I'm cool as long as you have the refrigerator."

"Okay, then we're set."

"Yes."

The television was set up first. After that, they got into a light-hearted conversation, stooped in nostalgia, reminiscing about childhood memories.

"Remember that Halloween when mom thought aliens were monitoring her? Hahahahaha! You were outside peeping in the window –"

"Yeah, and you were at the kitchen door... were we wearing masks?"

"No, remember, Noreen did those makeup jobs on us."

"That's rightttt... oh my god, that was so funny, Mom tried calling the police, and we had unplugged the telephone. Hahahahaha! That shit was hilarious! It went on for about what, an hour?"

"About 45 minutes, she went up and locked herself in her bedroom, after she couldn't find us. We were making noise downstairs, and Mom had to have been scared as fuck."

"Well yeah, she admitted she was, especially when we started turning the doorknob. But we let her off the hook when she started hollering. Remember, she started hollering that the police were coming. Oh my god, poor Mom. I miss her. What do you suppose she would be doing if she was alive?"

"I see her running a botanical garden, or doing something for animals, probably volunteering for something or another as long as it involved animals."

"Yeah… mom was the best."

Tyler had begun tearing into one of his muffuletta sandwiches. "We should have gotten beer," he said.

"Beer? Naaah, no beer. The sit-in will already be a mind-blowing situation. I don't want to add alcohol to the equation."

"No kidding, I wasn't thinking, well, it's about time I go in."

Jared checked his watch (it was 7:40 p.m.), and he nodded his head approvingly. "I hope we're wrong," he said.

Tyler simply smiled as he unlocked the cage to get in. "Well, at least I'll get some undisturbed rest, either way."

"I'll set the camera."

The evening had winded down uneventfully. It was now 8:49 p.m., and there was nothing to see here, Jared had convinced himself. He was happy that Tyler was sleeping comfortably, and the boring movie on the Syfy channel was having a similar effect on him.

He was about to dig in and call it a night until he heard Tyler twitching. He listened and slowly reared up. He witnessed Tyler experiencing spasms and convulsions, so he frantically went to the camera to make sure it was recording. Horrified and shaking, he managed to focus the camera, while it was on the tripod. Then he backed away. The sight that unfolded before his eyes were nothing short of incredulous. He saw his brother, a man he'd known all of his life, having involuntary and abnormal muscle contractions. His body sprouted hair as though the hair were shoots germinating after a period of dormancy. His mouth elongated into a snout as he stretched and snarled, baring his teeth while viciously growling. Gone was the hint of intelligent recognition – Jared was a stranger to him, a threat even, and he knew he would have severed his carotid artery if given a chance.

"Tyler... Tyler, it's me, brother," Jared said from a distance, but Tyler was too far absorbed by a primal instinct, an unalterable aptitude, clearly void of reason. It visibly bothered Jared to see his brother in this condition. Tyler was now virtually an animal – nothing more or less, and there was nothing anyone could've done about it.

Jared sat in a chair 5 feet away, monitoring his brother's aggression. He was more beast than man, unrecognizable in every sense, yet he stood upright, snarling, reaching out and trying to get a hold of anything. Jared could easily imagine him ripping someone apart. After a little more than 2 hours, he realized that his presence was causing Tyler chronic anxiety – he was relentless and had begun gnawing at the steel cage. Jared cried, turned off the television and left Tyler in the dark to his demons, before ascending the stairs.

CHAPTER 6

On Sunday, March 12th, the fog lifted, and in its wake was a crisp sunny day. Tyler was no worse for wear, but he'd fully recovered. Of course, he didn't remember anything, but the video would validate and fill in any missing parts. Jared slept better than he had in weeks, yet, the first part of the night was governed an unsettling dream. Like most of Jared's dreams, it made no sense, but he remembered being in a mountainous region, and druid priests or wizards were performing a ceremony of some sought at the base of a mountain. All wore robes and carried a staff. They were circled around what appeared to be the sacrifice, a young maiden, except when the subject reared up from her altar, the men acted as though they were her disciples, and she, their queer. She ordered a naked man to drink from a goblet, in which he did.

After the man drank from the goblet, he was no longer

a man, but more of a luminescent spirit, with stoic eyes as black as coal. Then the lady stood before the man and kissed him – at least Jared thought it was a kiss, but a vapor transferred from his mouth to hers, and the man collapsed to the ground, apparently dead. At that time, the druid priests uncovered their heads, and what Jared saw abruptly disturbed him and eventually woke him up from his sleep. All of the priests bore his image. They were all him!

He decided to go and look in on Tyler, who was going over the video.

"That can't be me, it looks nothing like me, it doesn't look human," he said, feigning denial. Jared looked on without saying anything. "I knew... I knew that it wasn't gonna be a pretty sight, but I would have never imagined. Look, I don't want anyone ever seeing me like this, you hear me? Ever!"

"Okay, I can't blame you. I understand, you know, you didn't recognize me when you changed."

Tyler ran his hand through his hair. "Sorry, man, I could've killed you, and not even remembered it. I can't be trusted around people in that state. I'm less than human. I'm an animal."

"I think you're too hard on yourself. It's not like you ever wanted this. You didn't ask for it – neither of us did. It's like you said, now that we know these transformations are taking place, we have to do everything to keep from harming people."

"I agree, at the very least, I can say I harmed nobody last night."

"Yes, you can. So it's a good start."

Tyler stopped looking at the video and laid the camera on his bed. "I had a crazy-ass dream this morning."

"A dream - what about?" Jared asked with heightened interest.

"Awww, it was nothing – couldn't make any sense of it... I was in the Caucasus Mountains – Mt. Elbrus to be precise, and these weird people were having some type of ceremony. Hell, where the hell is the Caucasus Mountains? I've never heard of them."

"Get the hell outta here - that's impossible! Was there something like a priestess or sorceress performing a ceremony with a naked guy who absorbed his energy?"

Tyler looked at Jared with a big-eyed expression. "Whoa, how did... was I talking in my sleep? How the fuck did you know that?!"

"Because I had the same dream - swear to god!"

"Wow, never heard of that before, not even from twins. What do you suppose it means?"

"I dunno. Were you able to finish the dream? I woke up from mine."

"Yeah, I think. Where did you leave off?"

"Let's see, well, I saw the part when she drained the guy's energy... I woke up at the part where the men around her took off their hoods, and all of them looked like me," Jared said.

"Like you? Hell, they all looked like me!" Tyler said. "They had my face."

"Some weird shit, but finish telling me."

"After that, there was a fire ceremony, and the priestess walked through the fire but didn't burn, not even her clothes, or what lil' clothes she had on... I don't remember anything after that. I think I woke up."

"Man, that's too surreal... too weird. Remember what that lady said – about looking for signs? Well, I think it's a sign, but I don't know what it means. You think Watson would know?" Tyler said.

"I seriously doubt it. Dream interpretation is out of his realm, but he probably knows who can interpret it."

"Let's go by and check him out. I need to go by there anyway."

"Gentlemen, gentlemen, gentlemen, it's going to storm today. What have I done to be so blessed by your presence?" Watson said, giving Jared and Tyler big generous hugs. "How did you bribe Tyler to come here?"

"Food, I offered to buy him lunch. You know how much this kid likes to eat," Jared said. "So how's it going, WW?"

"Well, a couple of things. For one, I've been answering questions for the police all morning,"

"The police?"

"Yeah, it seems we have a girl missing... I believe you were quite fond of the girl if I'm not mistaken."

"Who?" Jared asked as if he didn't know.

"Nayla Lloyd, one of my best designers."

"Nayla's missing?"

"Yes, according to her parents. She's been mia for about a week - about the same time for work. I told them all that I knew, which isn't much."

Jared looked over at Tyler, who was pretending to search for a name on his cell phone. "That's too bad... it's a shame. I hope she shows up. I was trying to hook up with her, you know, take her out for dinner or something. Such a pretty girl."

"You young people got ants in your pants, can't sit still for anything. She's probably cooped-up with some character, and he's spitting a yawn in her ear. It's too bad. She was very talented."

"She didn't strike me as that type... too smart for that nonsense, but I hope she shows up."

"Me too... you know, we're starting on two projects later this week - breaking grounds on the Prescott building and the new arena."

"Oh yeah, that's right, that new Montgomery Arena... supposed to hold a hundred and fifty thousand."

"You want us to be present?"

"It would be nice, but not necessary, besides you boys have got a lot on your plate as is... so what brings you in today?"

"Well, remember when you said to always keep you in the loop – to let you know when anything's happening first?"

"I do."

"That's what we are doing."

"Okay, am I gonna need to hear this news with a drink, or what?"

"Oh no, no, no - nothing like that... it's just that; we've been dreaming."

"Okay, been dreaming, huh?" Watson asked, looking at the brothers as if they had mental issues.

"Yeah... Tyler, you wanna tell him?"

"No, you're doing fine, you've already started."

Jared began telling Watson about the dream, while Watson poured himself a drink. As was his custom, Watson sat at the corner of his desk and listened on carefully. Even when Watson wasn't particularly always interested in anything the boys had to say, he pretended he was. Jared and Tyler appreciated that.

"And you say you both had the same dream?"

"Yes, the very same, and stop looking at us that way, we're serious. Do you think Lady 'What's-her-name' could interpret the dream, tell us what's going on?"

"Perhaps, I think if she can't, nobody can... I can call her guys, but you two are going to have to talk to her because you had the dream, not me,"

"That's not a problem,"

"Let's see... It's 1:13 p.m. here, so it should be about 7:13 p.m. over there. That's still a decent hour," Watson said, referring to his Rolodex."

"Okay, let's rock."

When Watson called Lady Dautbegovic, it was as if they were old friends, pleasantries and polite rhetoric peppered the conservation. Jared and Tyler waited patiently while the two chatted before Watson eventually handed Jared the phone.

"Hello?"

"Hello, young man. Mr. Watson tells me you and your brother have been experiencing the same dream," Lady Dautbegovic said.

"Yes, It only happened one time."

"Care to tell me what it was about?"

Jared told her about the dream – every aspect. He even said to her that he didn't finish his dream, but had to rely on Tyler's version and that his version omitted to show him the exact mountain's location, but Tyler's version did.

"That's because he is the older brother. His dream would be more detailed than yours."

"So you know what this is about?"

"I have an idea…"

Jared didn't say a word. He waited on her to continue.

"This can only mean that Asyla has risen… may God be with us all."

"Asyla?"

"Yes. Your dream was only a summons of sorts. There are others like you, who had the very same dream – Asyla's would-be followers."

By now, Watson had put the call on speaker so that everyone was listening.

"So, what does this mean?" Watson asked.

"Nothing," Lady Dautbegovic said. "Chances are, she's too far away to present a real threat to you. But your only chance for reversing the curse is to get close enough to her, or better yet, find Abigail whenever she wakes."

"You said that Abigail wakes up five days after Asyla. So will we hear from Abigail In the same manner?"

"I would say yes. Remember, you are connected to both Asyla and Abigail in the same manner. So chances are, you will be summoned the very same way," Lady Dautbegovic said.

"What do you suggest we do from here?" Jared asked.

"Boys, I want you to think of this as making a choice. You can choose to do nothing, and simply deal with your current status quo, or you can choose to answer one of their summonses. I will say that this is essentially the same old good versus evil tale that's been told in the Christian bible for centuries, but it's so much more than that. Asyla has many charms, and she will offer the things that mean most to you, but remember, her gifts are only tools in aiding her chance for longevity. Her purpose is to extend her life before she has to go back to sleep. Her main goal is to walk the earth forever without having to sleep. I hope you make the right choice for the world's sake.

"So, you think we should answer Abigail's summon?"

"I can't choose for you, because there are consequences – no matter the choice. But your lives are going to be affected, regardless.

"We understand," Jared said.

Jared and Tyler had just left the office, thinking about what Lady Dautbegovic had said.

"So, what do you think? Think we should make a move?"

"… and do what? I think we should wait as she said, and see if we hear from Abigail."

"Then?" Jared asked.

"Then, we make a move to find Abigail."

"Oh, just like that? Shouldn't we think of a game plan before heading into something we know nothing about? And who's to say we should respond to Abigail's summon? Lady D was very ambiguous about Abigail's motives. Asyla's motives are clear, but she hardly mentioned Abigail's," Jared said.

"She explained it earlier if you'd been paying attention, you'd already know that Abigail is the keeper of the Sacred Amulet. She's the "good witch', so to speak, just to put it in a perspective that you can understand. Asyla needs that amulet to obtain omnipotent powers. With it, she doesn't have to sleep. She could walk the earth and cause havoc at all times, like forever! She could be even more powerful than she already is, got it?"

"You're funny, man. I already knew all of that. I was referring to Lady Dautbegovic mentioning Asyla's motive, and not Abigail's. I just don't like jumping into anything. I mean, if we find Abigail, then what? Is she going to reverse the curse? Are we supposed to fight Asyla with her? What are we to do?"

"I don't know, even if we had a plan, I still wouldn't

know. J... look, we have time, and we have money. I can't think of anything better than the pursuit of getting rid of this curse. I can't live this way. I'm willing to do anything to rid myself of this shit! If we hear from Abigail, I think the next move is to find her, wherever she's at and do whatever it takes. Can you live the rest of your life the way you are? Chances are, we both have blood on our hands. I can't continue to live that way. I can't."

"You are right. I feel the same. I'm willing to do whatever it takes..." The two bumped fists.

Jared and Tyler lived 18 miles from the firm and the city, so they decided to load up on beverage and alcohol.

"I was kinda glad Watson didn't pressure us on Nayla's disappearance," Jared said.

"Why would he? He's in the blind like everyone else."

"Yeah, I guess you're right."

CHAPTER 7

It didn't take long for the second dream to occur. Six days after having the dream about Asyla, Jared and Tyler both experience the same dream again. This time, the vision was more ambiguous. The scene was at Ojos Del Salado, part of the Andes mountain range in Argentina and Chile. Three people were chanting around an open fire, again in a cave, similar to the tale that Lady Dautbegovic had told of Abigail, Elex, and Ira. They chanted in an old Anglo-Saxon language, but Jared and Tyler could understand them. There was a strange mist behind them as they held high a crystal ornament that, strangely enough, glowed brilliantly without a power source. Then the three took on a ghostly luminescence before pillowing into a large cloud that dispersed and changed into doves that flew north, east, west. Admittedly, this signaled the awakening of Abigail.

Early the very next morning, Tyler sat at the kitchen

table, contemplating their next move, when Jared came down the stairs.

"Good Morning, bro," Tyler said, sipping his coffee.

"G' morning... did you..."

"Yes... saw it too, in the Andes Mountains range, in Argentina and Chile. Again, don't know what it meant, other than announcing she had awakened."

"Abigail?"

"Yes, it has to be. It can be no one else, only this time, we don't have to concert with Lady Dautbegovic or Watson. Argentina is our next destination. Before it's all over, we will have logged as many miles as Pops used to do, remember?" Tyler said.

"Yep, I remember those days... but Watson will want to know about this. He might want to come along."

"Of course, and we will tell him," Tyler said. "But he doesn't have to come along and hold our hands like frightened little boys. Watson's getting up there in age. We will probably be moving at a fast pace. There's no telling where we'll have to go, what we'll have to do. Besides, who's going to run the business?"

"True, but I'll leave that up to him," Jared said.

The truth was, while Tyler's personality was sometimes aloof and reserved, Jared was the more gregarious and affable of the two. He was more extroverted and had always been the closer of the two boys to Watson. Even when their parents were alive, Jared made certain that Watson was included in the family outings and vacations. So, of course, if Watson wanted to come, he would be more than welcome, but it would be his choice, not Tyler's.

"Well you're gonna be responsible for his safety and him keeping up."

"Duly noted."

AFTER TELLING Watson about the latest dream, it was apparent to them he'd rather not join them in their forthcoming adventure, which wasn't a great concern. Jared always felt comfortable with him around, but he would adjust.

"These old bones ain't what they used to be. I'm afraid I would slow you boys down," Watson said, while Tyler glanced over, making sure Jared knew he was right. "I'm just used to waking up in my own bed these days, will be 60 next month. I'm afraid my adventure-seeking days are over."

"Awww, you sure WW? There's always a spot open for you," Jared said. "It's not gonna be the same without you."

Watson chuckled. "I appreciate that, young man. If you were going to the countryside, within the United States, I would consider it. But I think I will have to sit this one out. I just want you guys to be careful. I know why you feel you must go, but all of this dealing with mojos and the occult has got me on edge."

Jared and Tyler laughed.

"... I mean, really, you don't know what you're going up

against. You don't know who you're meeting - somebody that died in the 3rd or 4th century. You both could be heading towards a black hole, for all you know! Wanna think about this a little more?" Watson asked.

"No, we have thought about it," said Tyler. Neither one of us wants to live like this. It's pure hell. We have an idea of what must be done. We don't want to sit around and face a situation where we destroy somebody, or they destroy us," Tyler said. Tyler, more so than Jared, had been affected by his transformation. He had a seething determination for that never to happen again.

"I understand... just see if you can buy a gun once you get over there. I'm not sure of what use it'll be, but I'd feel better with you having it, then not."

"Alright, WW."

"And Tyler, pull your damn pants up, son! What's wrong with you, boy?"

"Alright, alright... I just couldn't find my belt this morning."

"No, you were like this one other time, when you came by recently. You're worth millions, and this is the best fashion statement you can come up with? Geez, son."

Jared laughed. "Well WW, you hold down the fort for us."

"I always do. I want you boys to be safe and careful," Watson said while corralling both brothers by the shoulder. "I want both of you coming back home to me, you hear?"

"Yessir, you know we will."

"Okay," he said, patting their shoulders. "Okay... then it's settled."

The airline, Aeromexico, was full, to Jared and Tyler's surprise. Neither figured that this many people would be flying to Argentina at the same time. Their first-class booking didn't seem to make a difference because people were continually using the restrooms, which were situated just behind their closed curtain.

"Must be a trendy destination," Tyler said.

"Must be, but I think this flight stops in Mexico before continuing to Argentina. Check the tickets."

"You're correct, it does. Hopefully, it'll alleviate some of the crowd."

"It's not that bad," Jared said. "You better be glad you didn't go to Vancouver with Watson and me last year. First-class was booked, so we had to take the economy, and I was sitting in the middle seat next to Watson and this lady who had to use an oxygen respirator. And get this – she wanted to sit next to the window! I was uncomfortable the whole flight."

"Damn, so I guess I shouldn't complain, huh?"

"No. Keep your mouth shut."

The brothers laughed.

The rest of the trip was filled with the brothers laughing at Watson and their daily hijinks. They both seem to take exceptional delight with dissecting and denouncing Hollywood's take on monsters, especially vampires and werewolves.

"So, you're not affected by daylight – not in the sense that you can't function?" Tyler asked Jared.

"No, it's daylight now... I mean, I'm a little more sensitive, but I have no trouble functioning."

"What about garlic and crosses?"

"No affect. I don't like garlic, so I rarely eat it, but crosses don't bother me."

"Okay, I bet holy water burns you."

"Hahahaha! What the fuck is holy water? I've never been around the stuff. I wouldn't know."

"… and reflections, can you see yourself in the mirror?"

"Hell yeah! Remember, you were with me. I just saw myself this morning, for Christ's sake! All that stuff is bullshit. It makes the vampire more compelling and interesting. I don't see myself as a vampire. I've been afflicted with the rare need and carving for blood to survive, but all that other garbage is just that – garbage!" Jared said.

"Well, for you, maybe, but most of the superstitions about werewolves are fairly right on, as you have witnessed. I transform doing every full moon, which is roughly twelve times a year, and I think a silver bullet will kill me. I also have superhuman strength, speed, and agility. All true."

"I think the difference is that vampires are derived from mythology, whereas werewolves' origins are derived from folklore," Jared said.

"Tell me, what's the difference?" Tyler asked. "… because I don't see a difference."

Jared thought for a minute, then admitted, "I don't know… but you've gotta admit; it was a cool thing to say."

The brothers laughed.

The restless ruckus had settled, and the two napped until they were a few miles within their destination. Jared pushed Tyler, as he had begun to snore.

"Wake up, sleeping beauty, you're starting to slobber."

Tyler readjusted but continued with his nap.

Jared reached overhead to gather his notepad from his luggage. He checked on the hotel they had booked, talking as he typed, "the… Ritz…Carlton… Alcalde 15, Santiago, Chile…". Chile? He thought they were supposed to be heading to Argentina?!

"Tyler, Tyler, wake up… wake up, buddy. Tyler stirred. "I thought we were supposed to be flying to Argentina? Our hotel is in Chile!"

"Huh?"

"Chile, our hotel is in Chile!"

"So. Chile, Argentina, it's all the same. We are going to land in Argentina, then drive to Chile."

Jared had an astounding expression on his face.

"What? They are close to each other. Chile is next to Argentina, and even more important it's right by the Andes Mountains region. Don't you know anything about geography?"

"Well, I just didn't know where Chile was, I've never

been to this part of the world," Jared admitted, embarrassingly.

"Neither have I, but I know where certain countries are located on the map," Tyler said.

"Okay, asshole. You don't have to be a jerk about it."

Tyler smiled. "Trust me. I hear Chile has some great beaches, plus the women are hot - not that we'll have time to partake of the delicacies.

"Nope, we're gonna take care of business first, maybe afterward," Jared said.

"Agreed."

ARGENTINA WAS BEAUTIFUL, but so was Santiago, Chile. Its dynamic cultural landscape was bursting with energy, a city of syncopated cultural currents, world-class chefs, madhouse parties, expansive museums, and top-flight restaurants. It boasted sidewalk eateries, cafes, and beer halls, as well as a historical architecture scene and a bevy of hillside parks. In short, Santiago was an old-guard city on the cusp of a modern-day renaissance. It was precisely Jared and Tyler's kind of place.

It was now April 4th. The weather was crisp and cool, somewhat cooler than Jared and Tyler imagined it would be. They later found out that they were near the beginning of the fall in Chile. Since Chile was in the southern hemisphere, its weather is the exact opposite of the United States, which is in the northern hemisphere. The locals said it would get no higher than 70 degrees, the low 47 degrees. So the present temperature was comfortable, actually, but being near the mountains kept the city 5 degrees cooler than the rest of the country. The brothers would have to invest in a coat. Still, first, they needed to explore finding a mountain guide, which shouldn't be a problem since guided expeditions, mountaineering, and trekking were the chief tourist attractions amongst things to do in the city.

"So hiking and mountain climbing is huge in this city?" Jared asked Joaquin Olivares, their bartender, as they sat at the trendy *Focaccia Bar & Restaurant*.

"Yes," said Joaquin, a native of Argentina, but had studied at Rutgers University in the states. "See those mountains over there, they generate and dictate a lot of what goes on around here - kind of like a fishing village."

"I see, so we should have no trouble finding a mountain guide?"

"Oh God, no. They're everywhere, probably one or two in here as we speak," Joaquin assured them. May I ask, what brings you to Santiago to hike? It's not exactly the first destination for brothas."

"You mean, no blacks come here!" Tyler feign surprised. Joaquin smiled. "But seriously, are there no black people around here?"

"None to speak of, which means a tiny percentage that is integrated with the general population. Americans and Canadians are well-liked here, be they black or white. The only people that are looked done upon are the Bolivians and the Peruvians. Oh, and they're not that fond of people from other Latin countries, except maybe the upper-class people from Argentina, Uruguay, and Brazil."

"Wow!" Jared and Tyler laughed. "One has to carry around a chart to see if they're on the "liked" list around here – or the hated."

Joaquin laughed heartily and said, "people are fickle; the same, no matter where you go."

"You can say that again. We certainly have our share of racism in the states."

"Yes, I've heard. That was one of the reasons I decided not to live in the states, but there's no escaping it. It's just as bad here, but you didn't answer my question."

"Which was?"

"Your reason for coming here."

"Oh yeah, sorry," Tyler said. "We are here…"

"… because it was something we promised our father," Jared said, finishing Tyler's sentence. He wasn't sure what Tyler would've said and felt Joaquin didn't need to know the real reason they were there. "Our father is deceased, so it was a request by him. The Andes are considered one of the new modern-day marvels of the world. We promised our dad that we would try to visit the 'not-so-traveled-paths'. A bucket list for us, of sorts., to honor our father."

"I can relate. Sorry to hear about your dad, but I understand. It was one of the reasons I studied in the states. My father wanted me to see the rest of the world, 'don't build on a grounded stone,' he would always say."

"Exactly! So, I take it you're from an affluent family."

"You can say that I guess. But as you see, I'm part of the working class now. So your father, did he specifically say the Andes?"

"As a matter of fact, he did, among other places."

"Hmm, probably because the Andes Mountains region is the largest in the world."

Jared and Tyler looked at each other. "You say what?"

Joaquin repeated himself, then asked, "so which mountains are you climbing?"

"Well, we didn't plan on climbing any mountain. We were thinking of more like hiking."

"Okay… just any area?"

Tyler looked through his phone. He had actually saved the name of the mountain region. "It's this one, I can't pronounce it," he said, holding the phone close enough to show Joaquin.

"Ohhh, It's called the **Nevado Ojos del Salado,** but we drop "Nevado" and simply call it **Ojos del Salado** or the Big Scotchy or Old Salty around here… you do know it's a live volcano, don't you?"

"It's what? Are you kidding?!" The brothers said in shock, almost in exact unison.

"Yes… I thought you knew. Not only is it active, but it's the highest active volcano in the world."

"What?! I'm not hiking no goddamn active volcano!" Tyler shouted, his stomach starting to turn. "We came all this way for nothing!"

"Awww, it's safe… it hasn't been active in over a thousand years. However, there was a report that some bubbling was going on in 1993, but the chance of it erupting is highly remote. Really, it's highly unlikely," Joaquin said, smiling.

Jared was still no less shocked. He held his beer close to his mouth, but wasn't drinking, nor did he utter a word. He was speechless.

"So when was the last time it was hiked?" Tyler asked.

"I don't know, probably yesterday. People go up there all the time... it's the main climbing destination around these parts. Like I've said, the mountain is safe, or I wouldn't be living here."

"We feel better now, right, Tyler?" Jared said, forcing himself to make light of the situation. Tyler sat dejected, disappointed, even though his hopes weren't completely extinguished. Things just hadn't panned out the way he'd hoped for, though he'd had no plans.

"We should've planned better, should've done some research. Hell, any research. We have gotta think things over," Tyler said.

"Sorry, man," Joaquin said.

"Nooooo, it's not your fault. We're grateful having met you and you informing us on what we needed to know. We appreciate it. Thank you."

Joaquin poured the two more beers. "Here, these are on the house."

"Thanks, man."

CHAPTER 8

The brothers came back to their hotel room to regroup and change clothes. Their spirits were down, but they were still determined to make it a successful trip. They were just going to have to figure out another way.

"Okay, let's figure out what we do know—# 1. We know we are looking for Abigail & company. #2. We both know Abigail is somewhere in that mountain, right?"

"Right."

"#3. We know that we will have to come to her, she's not coming to us. #4. We know that neither of us is experienced hikers and #5. We both know that mountain climbing is out. It's non-negotiable!" Tyler said.

"Right, right, and a big right... So what are you proposing?"

"Hmmm, I don't rightfully know. Hiking seems the most viable option..."

"Unless..."

"Unless what?"

"Unless we use a helicopter," Jared said. "We've both seen that place in the dream. We don't know the exact location, but wherever it was, it seemed flat enough for a helicopter to land there."

"That's it!" Tyler grabbed his brother and kissed his forehead. "That's the answer! We will hire someone with a helicopter and see if there are places up there to land. You're beautiful lil' bro. Have I ever told you that?"

"No, and make sure you never tell me again!"

Tyler laughed. "We can go look into that when we go back out."

"Actually, we can do it now. We have the internet, you know."

"I knew that; I just thought you wanted to explore more of the city while we are here."

"I'm good," Jared said, surprising Tyler. "I just wanna get this behind me. I can't concentrate on anything else."

"I'm feeling you, lil' bro. Okay, look for a helicopter service while I take a quick shower."

"K, I'm on it."

It didn't take long for Jared to find his source. He found two helicopter touring services nearby, with both specializing in private tours. He decided to wait on Tyler, before proceeding.

Since both companies were nearby, the brothers decided to visit them.

. . .

THE FIRST WAS a place called *Helix Copter*. It specialized in private tours, as advertised, but was on a fixed schedule and usually preferred a group minimum of 4 people for $650, and you toured as a group with a mountain guide. The second place was *Rototec,* located just 35 minutes from the Andes. It could provide a private mountain guide for a two-person minimal tour. The cost wasn't a factor, but it was for only $200 per person with the guide, $175 without the guide.

"So say we preferred a guide for an indefinite amount of time, say two days, maybe three... could you provide such a service?" Tyler asked the thin caramel-colored man, Jose.

"I'm sure we can, but I have to run it by the boss first."

"Is he here? Can we speak to him?"

"Sure, he's with a customer right now, but he should be available shortly. Have a seat."

"Thanks." Jared and Tyler looked at each other without saying a word. Seven minutes later, they were introduced to the owner.

"Nice to meet you. I'm Emmanuel, Manny, for short."

"A pleasure, Manny," they said, shaking his hands. "I'm Jared, and this is my brother, Tyler."

"Fellows... hear you want to rent a 'copter for a couple of days."

"Yes, we were hoping that could be possible."

"Oh, I think we can make it happen if money isn't an issue. It just depends on the availability of the pilot, but most of them are motivated by money."

"Money's no issue," Jared said.

"Okay, and you will have to sign a waiver. You can buy insurance, but that's optional," Manny said, handing each a clipboard.

"So, does $400 a day sound reasonable?"

"Yes, of course."

"Fine, and oh, the pilot does accept tips, Manny said, smiling. "When will you need the 'copter?"

Jared looked at Tyler. "I guess tomorrow, right?"

"Yes, tomorrow. We can start early, say, 10:00?"

Jared laughed at Tyler's perception of early. "Let's try for 8:00 a.m., ten's a little late to start, I think. You cool with that?"

"Yeah, I guess," Tyler said, unenthused. He was not an early riser.

"Okay, then eight it is. I'll make sure it's ready for tomorrow, do you have any questions?"

"Uhhh, yes. What if we want to keep the 'copter longer?"

Manny grinned. "I have your credit card on file. Oh, one more thing. I almost forgot to tell you; you're responsible for the pilot's food and any other expenses."

"Kinda figured as much," Tyler smiled.

APRIL 5TH DIDN'T START WELL. Jared had just got off the phone, talking with Watson. It appeared that the police had been by, further inquiring about the whereabouts of Nayla Lloyd. Jared hadn't thought of her of late, but now, here he was, flooded with emotions. It was a good thing from that perspective that he had his current problems to keep him concerned. Being responsible for someone's death leaves an open laceration on one's soul. It can never be closed. It can never be patched.

"Tyler, are you awake?"

"Grrr… I am now," Tyler said, stretching.

"It's 7 o'clock, time to get up."

"Hmmm… what time did we go to bed?"

"About 1:30 a.m. Hurry, get in the showers."

The helicopter was ready as promised, all cleaned, gassed up, and inspected. The pilot, a spunky little curmudgeon, was a man of few words, which suited the brothers fine. The less they had to explain, the better for all.

"Hey guys, got a good man for you, and he's free for almost 4 days. I like for you to meet Ricardo Gutierrez, we all call him "Pez" around here," Manny said.

The brothers shook his hands. "I'm Jared, and this is Tyler."

Pez nodded approvingly.

"Why do they call you, Pez?"

"You ever heard of the candy, Pez? Wanna show 'em, Pez?

Pez reached in his pockets and pulled out two Pez dispensers.

"You only have two today? I swear, this guy has about, what – 200, 300 Pez dispensers. He's always eating 'em. I've never seen him without them," Manny said.

Pez smiled and proudly corrected Manny. "I have close to 400 dispensers. I collect them by the series."

"The series?"

"Si, you know, like… I got the SuperHero series, the Star Wars series, the Harry Potter series, etc. They accumulate faster that way."

"Got 'cha!" Jared said. He could easily see that the candies were Pez's passion, however strange, but he wasn't there to judge. He was anxious to get loaded and explore their strange and bizarre adventure. He had never flown in a helicopter, so he wasn't sure what to expect. Tyler, too, seemed anxious and excited. Before long, they were up and on their way.

Flying in a helicopter was quite different from flying in an airplane. The brothers enjoyed the broader aerial view and how the aircraft was able to pivot left or right, up or down. They liked the helicopter's ability to hover over one area, in one spot, something an airplane was incapable of doing. Still, this didn't mean that helicopters were better than a winged aircraft, they were just better for this particular kind of outing.

"So Pez, how long did it take you to master flying a helicopter?" Jared asked.

"Oh, about 51 hours."

"That's it?!"

"Si, that's it, my friend."

"I thought you needed about 1,000 to 1,500 hours under your belt."

"Si, but that's for commercial pilots, the ones who fly for passenger airlines."

"Okay, gotcha... So do you do that, or has ever flown commercially?"

"No. It's always been helicopters. We are two different creatures. I mean, it's not unheard of, but people who like flying helicopters don't enjoy flying airplanes; two different disciplines are involved. For one, flying a helicopter is harder. You can't put a helicopter on auto-pilot. And I don't enjoy flying straight lines over 25,000 and 30,000 feet in the air."

"I see. I never considered that, well, which one pays the best? I'm considering doing it, especially if I only have to put in 50 hours. You think I can do this, Tyler?"

"No."

"Fuck you!"

Pez got a chuckle out of the brothers' antics. "They both pay well... including tips, I made close to 100k last year, and I only work full time during the busy season."

"When's that?"

"Starting now, the spring and summer months."

"Sounds like a winner to me. I'm going to look into it when I get back home. I'm serious. It's something I want to do."

"Si. So what do you do for a living?"

"My brother and I are into architecture," Jared said, handing Pez one of his business cards.

"*Jace & Jace Architects,* so you guys design buildings?"

"Something like that, we are co - CEOs of the firm."

"You're kind of young to be CEOs."

"Our father owned the place… we inherited it."

"So, your father's deceased?"

"Yes."

"Sorry to hear."

"It's okay. It's been a while, and we've adjusted. How old are you, and do you have any siblings?"

Pez popped a couple of candies from his Pez dispenser. "I'm 35, and I have two sisters. I'm the middle child."

"Ayyy, the man of the house."

"Yes, I am."

"Well that's good, Pez. So, why are you so quiet, Tyler?"

"I'm just enjoying the view. Are there good places to land in the mountains?" Tyler inquired.

"Si, actually lots. There's a little store at the base, on the east side. A good place to lodge is Hostel Campo Base. I know the lady that runs it. You can also stay at Hotel Municipal, although it's a little expensive."

"People are living up here?"

"Si… si senor, many. not so much in the steep mountains, but on the hilly flatter areas, especially in Peru."

"Yes, I remember talking about the indigenous people of Peru in school… never thought I'd be in their backyard."

"So what brought you guys here, I mean, you say you're

not mountaineers, right? You're not serious hikers, just wondering."

Jared looked over his shoulder at Tyler, who subtly nodded.

"Pez, you wouldn't believe it if we told you," Jared said.

"Try me."

"No, we can't."

"Are you searching for gold?"

"Gold?" Jared laughed. "I wished it was that simple."

"Oh, I get it... you guys are doing that spiritual awakening stuff. I bought a couple from Italy up here, doing the same thing. I could've told them. They can find that in their backyard. I could've saved them coming 8,000 miles," Pez laughed, along with the brothers.

Pez wasn't the silent grouch that he was perceived. Instead, he was uniquely introspective, affable, and candid.

"You're kinda right. We are definitely on a soul-searching journey. So, what's that down there?" Jared said, pointing, trying to direct Pez to another topic.

"That's a salt basin... a little salt pond. You are going to found 'em everywhere, formed from the volcano."

"This volcano, we heard that it's safe, right?"

"Si amigo, it is... It hasn't erupted in over 1,300 years, but still listed as an active volcano - actually, it's the tallest active volcano in the world."

"Yes, we heard, and this mountain range is the biggest, right?"

"Correct. I think it expands over 7 South American

countries; they are Colombia, Ecuador, Venezuela, Peru, Argentina, let's see, Chile, and I'm missing one."

Tyler checked his cell phone, and said, "You're missing, uhh…here it is… Bolivia."

"That's right, Bolivia."

"Yeah, I'd say that's pretty big!"

CHAPTER 9

The brothers both agreed that **Hostel Campo Base** was too far and too rudimentary, far from their taste. They opted for the much closer (and newly renovated) **Hotel & Casino Antay** in nearby Copiapo, Chile, which was only 9 miles from their destination.

Like anywhere, getting access to the mountains required some formalities. Jared and Tyler learned that they had to register and inform the Chilean police department, CONAF (the National Forest Corporation). They also needed to notify the Atacama Sernatur (the Chilean tourism service) before any hiking, trekking or mountain climbing, which was conveniently located at **Nevado de Tres Cruces National Park,** where **Ojos del Salado** resided.

As luck would have it, the park had a large clearing for

helicopters to land, but some hiking was necessary, to Jared's and Tyler's chagrin.

"Awww, it's not that bad," Tyler said. "Your lazy butt could use some exercise."

"Lazy? I know you're not talking. At least I'm a member at a health club."

"It doesn't matter if you never go to it."

Jared gave Tyler the evil eye.

"Hey guys, this is the route we shall take," Pez interrupted, showing the two a map. "We are starting here at Copiapó, then to Laguna Verde… we can take the route through the Paipote Valley, or we can go here, through the Andres Valley," he said, pointing to the spots on the map.

"Which is better? I mean, looking at this, it means nothing to us. Which is the fastest way? Where is the closest place to land the helicopter, to the mountain?"

"Probably the Atacama Refuge, maybe even as close as the Tejos Refuge, where the elevation of the mountain itself starts, but you're going to bypass the best part of the journey," Pez said.

Jared looked at Tyler, then at Pez. "Look, Pez, I guess it's our fault that we didn't explain this better to you. Our bad. We're not interested in hiking or trekking across the Andes. We are looking for something. We don't know what it is, but we'll know when we find it. I'm sorry, but we can't explain it any other way. The quicker we find it, the quicker we can return home or just hang out for a while. But we must take care of this first. It's something we must do."

"Si señor, I understand. Forgive me."

"No, no... you've done nothing wrong. We should've explained our mission better. That's on us, not you," Tyler said, while Jared nodded.

"Si, but regardless of your reasons, there are some steps required before attempting to travel at such high altitude. You need to acclimate your bodies for the elevation. I still think it's a good idea to stop by Laguna Verde first before proceeding."

"Okay. We have supreme confidence in you, Pez. Hell, we have no other choice," Jared admitted.

"Good, so we are going to need a flashlight, water, gloves, sunglasses, coats, and maybe a couple of tents, if we decide to camp overnight, oh, and whatever snacks you want, and you might want to bring some swimming trunks."

"Swimming trunks? But, I thought this was understood, this isn't a..?"

"No problem," Jared said, finishing Tyler's sentence.

"Just trust me. So, gentlemen, let's get this underway, shall we?"

"T'ain't no time like the present," Jared said.

After gathering and loading the supplies, it was merely a matter of satisfying their latest hunger urges, and sampling some of Chile's finest beers. The time was 2:20 p.m., a little late for mountain trekking, but what did Jared and Tyler care? They viewed it as being hours ahead of tomorrow, so no problem.

Their first destination would be Laguna Verde.

THE RHYTHMIC SOUND of the helicopter's rotary blades hummed in the pristine air. The weather was stark, wild, and windy, with temperatures hovering above 55 degrees. As they approached a body of water, the men could barely make out what appeared to be some type of pink vegetation. It wasn't until the helicopter landed that they realized it was a large group of flamingos feeding on the plankton, green algae, and krill-rich crustaceans that were grouped like pink pearls in the turquoise-green lagoon. The backdrop of the nearby mountains, white terrain, and navy-blue skies gave the lake a surreal jaw-dropping decor.

"Wow, I've never seen anything like this," Tyler marveled.

"Me neither. This place is like another planet - beautiful, but weird as fuck, and oddly bizarre."

"Gentlemen, welcome to Laguna Verde. You're about 14,200 feet above sea level, one of the more beautiful spots you'll encounter in route to Ojos del Salado. I'm afraid the amenities are minimal, but there's a little camp about a hundred yards that way. Meanwhile, let's get out and stretch our legs."

Jared and Tyler walked about the strange land, exploring. They might as well have been on the moon because there was no other person around; besides the birds, there were no other life forms around.

"Hey, where is everybody?" Jared asked.

"It's actually normal for there to be six or fewer people up here. It's is a good time to trek the mountain. It's windy, but not too windy; cool but not too cold. I've seen both extremes before, and it's not pretty."

"I've noticed there aren't any other animals around, besides the flamingos. Is that because of the altitude?"

"There are small birds, along with the flamingos, you just can't see them. No, it's not because of the altitude, it's because the lake can be poisonous if you were to drink large consumptions. You can take a swim in it; it won't harm you. But my suggestion is not to drink it."

"Poisonous, huh?"

"These little white puddles of water you see here, and there are salt craters. The salt craters have various trace minerals, but they also contain traces of sulfur and arsenic in them because of the volcanoes. Arsenic is poisonous."

"Wow! So all this snow looking stuff around the lake is salt."

"Si, siii... It's salt, not snow. I don't know why the flamingos aren't affected, but they love this area, maybe because the waters are so warm in some places, and the food, of course.'

"Heeeeey, check this out!" Tyler said, approaching the skeletal remains of a cow. "This is cool."

"Kinda spooky to me... might be a bad omen," Jared echoed.

"That has been here for a long time, don't know how it got here, though. My theory is that some nomads came by, and this fellow wandered off and found out the hard way that the lake is poisonous."

"So Pez, how often do you come here?"

"Maybe once a month, on average. The Andes covers a large area, and my clients are always going to different mountain regions. This area is trendy, but remember, there are eleven other pilots where I work, and we all have various assignments around the Andes."

"Cool. So what is that, down there?" Jared said, pointing to a stony slope.

"That's where I'm taking you, you'll see."

The men walked upon what appeared to be a small cliff. Below was a wall of stones, arranged in concrete slabs, forming a headboard about four feet high over a natural pool of water.

"What are you doing?"

"C'mon, jump in," Pez said, stripping down to his shorts."

Jared and Tyler walked around the front of the jacuzzi-like pool of water and searched through their bags for the swimming shorts.

"So, where are we gonna change?"

"Here. I don't see any other people around, behind those rocks, you woozies."

Jared and Tyler reluctantly changed into their swimwear. The climate was arid and windy. There were no trees to speak of, and minimal vegetation to ever suggest that this was a viable ecosystem, but the place held its beauty, nonetheless. This was a special place on earth with the impressive Licancabur volcano in its backdrop, the elegant flamingos, and the azure sky.

"So, you're okay with this," Tyler asked Jared, before heading for the water.

"Of course, why wouldn't I be?"

"Hurry up, you guys! There's nothing to fear," said Pez, and he was right. The water was surprisingly warm, and the stones beneath their feet felt like smooth flower petals.

"Ouch, ouch, ouch… it's hot!"

"No, it's not. It's warm, it's a natural hot spring, from the volcano."

"From which volcano, the one we're going to?"

"I doubt it, probably from that one over there," Pez said, pointing to Licancabur. "Or one of the other mountains that's close by."

"This is nice, why didn't we bring beer?"

"There's some in the 'copter," Jared said, looking at Tyler.

"Who, me? I'm not going back to the 'copter!"

Jared and Pez laughed. "Why not? You were the last one in the water."

"So, why don't you go? You got in the water first."

"No, Pez did."

"Yeah Pez, you were in the water first."

Pez unceremoniously got out of the water, without saying a word, and headed for the helicopter, making the brothers feel small in their bickering.

"Damn, we should've gone for the beer. You play too much. I'm serious, man. There's a time for everything."

"No, you play too much, and you're starting to piss me off," Tyler said.

"Well, that's your problem," Jared retorted. He, too, was starting to get angry but realized being upset with his brother was the last thing they needed. "Look, I know you're under a lot of pressure – we both are but getting upset with one another is not going to solve anything. It's the last thing we need."

Tyler was quiet for a minute, then decided to put aside his petty anger.

"You're right, little bro. I guess I'm a little irritable? Have you had a vision, a dream? Anything?"

"No, nothing."

"I was hoping we would have seen some type of sign before now," Tyler said. "Maybe we shouldn't have come before receiving more information. We're here, but I feel lost as hell. I don't know what else to do."

"Maybe we have enough information, you know? Maybe we need to just go back over what we already know. But we just gotta have faith and push on."

Yeah, maybe you're right, little bro."

"Heeey, what's with this 'little bro' bullshit? I'm bigger than you."

"You're slightly taller by a half-inch, which isn't noticeable."

"And I outweigh you by 7 pounds."

"Hahahahahaha! So that's a bragging point for you? Really, Jared? Again, not noticeable."

"I'm just saying, stop calling me' little bro'. I hate that!"

"Okay, there's no reason to get all hostile. Don't get your panties in a wad, as Watson would say. Hey, Pez's coming back. By the way, how are you doing with your rabbit blood?"

Jared laughed. "It's cattle blood, and I'm doing okay."

"Just okay?"

"Well, it's an alternative, but I thirst more. A rare, juicy steak would hit the spot right now."

"I hear you."

"What day is the full moon for this month?"

Tyler didn't answer, Pez was back with the beer.

"Hey man, 'preciate it, but you didn't have to go for the beer. Tyler or I would've eventually gone."

"You would have? When?"

Jared and Tyler didn't answer. They were embarrassed. It wasn't until Pez popped some of his candy from one of his ridiculously designed dispensers and smiled, did they feel relieved.

"Hey, you go buy, I go fetch… no problem, amigo. I like this arraignment," Pez said.

Jared and Tyler laughed.

It was now 4:30 in the afternoon. The trio was basked in the hot spring bath, ate a fabulous gourmet meal (it was carry-out, courtesy of the hotel restaurant), and gathered their belongings. The next stop would be the Tejos Refuge.

CHAPTER 10

At 19,000 feet above sea level, The Tejos Refuge is a modest, well-insulated, orange, steel structure that served its purpose, which was to provide shelter in what could sometimes be harsh living conditions. With a bathroom, toilet, a bedroom with six beds, and a kitchen with a dining area, one could imagine this being one of the last true havens before braving the *Ojos del Salado.* The shelter wasn't so much a mountain hut as it was a sanctuary in the truest of sense.

Upon arriving, the trio was surprised to see two other hikers preparing to leave. They had spent the night, and one had taken ill, perhaps a victim of the high altitude. When hiking a peak like the Ojos del Salado, one has to expect close encounters such as this, because shelter was at a premium. Because of their wealth, Jared and Tyler were spared the trials of "roughing it" like a real mountaineer. It had taken the minimal effort to get to the point they were at, so they weren't tired or exhausted. They would stay at the refuse long enough to take a piss, on the outside, then move on.

It was 6:00 pm, still early but late for hiking. The temperature had dropped to 35 degrees, and the trio was now donning coats and hiking gear. They were exactly one hour behind the two men they had encountered but seeing them again was highly remote.

At the base of the mountain, the trio would make their first decision. The trio had approached a fork.

"Well, left or right, or do you want to continue circling the base before ascending?" Pez asked the two.

"Right," said Tyler. "When in doubt, always go right."

"Si, this part of the mountain is relatively easy to access. There are a few craters and boulders, but otherwise, you don't need any ropes, crampons, ice cleats, or ice axes, nothing like that. You don't even need gloves."

"Will the temperatures be getting any colder?"

"Probably, you're in the mountains. Everything up here fluctuates, one can never tell. Why? You look well insulated."

"Oh, I'm okay right now. Just was wondering, what's that smell?"

"Sulfur, you will smell a faint scent from time to time, depending on how the wind is blowing. It's from the volcano."

"I swear, the more I hear about this volcano, the farther I wish to be away from it. How can you guys go day to day, knowing there's an active volcano in your backyard, knowing this thing could blow at any time?" Tyler said.

"I guess we don't think about it. It's far enough away. Besides, there are worse things to think about and fear, besides the volcano."

"Yeah, like what?"

"Well, I fear not having the volcano around."

"Really?"

"Yes, of course, think about it. What would I do without the volcanoes and mountains? What kind of life would I have without the Andres attracting you adventure seekers, you tourists?"

"Yeah, I see what you mean. I guess it's all in one's perspective," Tyler said.

Forty-five minutes into the hike, the thin air had taken its toll. Jared and Tyler would have never guessed they would be winded this soon. There was less oxygen in the air at such high altitudes, because the higher one goes up from sea level, the atmospheric pressure is reduced, thus making it harder to breathe. And the less oxygen you get per breath, the harder your body works to make up the difference. The brothers were experiencing the very same symptoms that plagued one of the mountaineers back at the refuge.

They stopped to rest on a large border, eating beef jerky, trail mixes, and drinking mango and peach Snappers. The sun was setting, while the wind howled undauntedly throughout the desolate mountain. Pez sought a place to take a piss, which afforded Jared and Tyler time to figure out their next move.

"I've been thinking about what you said, you know, about going over the information in the dream," Tyler said.

"And what did you come up with?"

"Nothing. I wanted to get with you, see what you had."

Jared looked at him, puzzled. "What cha you mean?"

"Since we haven't had another dream, maybe it's like you said, we already have enough information," Tyler said. "Let's go over the dream together, one more time… now, it's safe to say we're at the right destination, wouldn't you agree?"

"Yes, the same mountain range, the same volcano… yes, I'm positive."

"Me too, can you think of anything that would help us narrow the exact location down, something we haven't thought about, anything?"

Jared thought for a minute, reflectively, and said, "No, I really can't. We both know Abigail was at a vacant spot, a large open cave. I can remember the amulet and the doves flying in various directions, same as you. Sorry."

"It's not your fault, just wish we had more to go on."

Jared looked on languidly, trying to remember.

"Pez must be taking a shit," Tyler laughed.

"Wait, I think I remember something," Jared said.

"You do? What?"

"A flag, a green flag at the cave entrance."

"You sure?"

"It was green or gray. I remember. I'm positive."

"Great Jared, great! That little detail could make the difference in us finding the location," Tyler said, high-fiving his brother. "I wonder why I can't remember it?"

"Your old, corroded brain needs lubricating," Jared said, laughing.

"You'd better be glad you came up with something," Tyler smiled.

Jared was having difficulties with the glare from the sun, reflecting off the snow. After resting and regaining their bearings, the trio moved forward, towards a relatively flatter part of the mountain. The crisp cleanness of the mountain air baptized all in its presence, and every elevation upwards was a discovery.

"What in the fuck is that? Are we still on earth?" Jared said, upon arriving at a plethora of strange ice structures. "What are these?"

"They're called 'penitentes'... nieves penitentes, to be precise. They're ice formations that you'll never see at lower sea levels. Kind of freaky, isn't it?"

"Wow. I've never seen anything like this, have you, Tyler?"

"Never, but I like it, it's like a football field of ice blades, ice soldiers."

"Si. These only form in high altitudes. Chances are,

most people will never see these unless they scale a mountain."

"What are they called, again?"

"Nieves penitentes."

"Nieves penitentes. Well, I've learned something new today. Cool," Tyler said.

"Should we move on, gentlemen?"

"Yes, but let me take a couple of pics. I want my pic with these. Those things are cool as fuck," Jared said.

"Here, give me the camera. I'll take some photos of both of you," said Pez.

"Cool!"

As the men pressed onward, the questioning persisted, even though it was getting later and darker.

"Pez, how high is this mountain?"

"It's estimated to be about 6,882 meters.

"Can you translate that into feet."

"Si, it's not the first time I've been asked that. It's 22,671 feet, give or take a foot."

"And how high are we now?"

"Oooh, I would say about 14,000 feet… maybe 15,000 feet. Are you planning on scaling the mountain, reaching the peak?"

"Oh, hell, no! Hopefully, we won't have to go much higher. I mean, it's been cool and all, but I don't plan on going to the top of this mug, it just depends."

"On what, amigo, if you don't mind me asking?"

"Well, Tyler and I believe we'll know that when we see an indicator," Jared said, looking back at Tyler.

Pez, understandably, didn't want to pry, but he was trying to comprehend what type of inner consciousness quest the brothers were attempting. Jared could sense Pez's trepidation, and to ease his mind, he decided to come clean and tell Pez part of the truth.

"Pez, this started when my brother and I had a dream… the very same dream."

"The same?"

"Yes, identical."

"That's weird. Are you guys twins?"

"No, Tyler is a year and a half older than me, but can you understand why we thought that someone, here in the Andes, was trying to tell us something? We had never had the same dreams before then, in fact, it has happened twice!"

"Wow, amigo! Yes, I do understand. If I had the money, I would do just as you and your brother."

"See, I told Tyler you would understand! He was afraid you would think we were crazy or something."

"Noooo, it's perfectly normal. What's not normal is dreaming the same dream. That would spook the hell out of me," Pez said.

"Exactly! That's why we're here. It must be an omen or something. What do you think?"

"Oh, I don't know, amigo. I come from a culture of many myths, many omens – nothing proven to be true. I'm not like the rest of my fellow countrymen. I'm not ruled by superstition. I couldn't tell you."

"Aha! A man of science. I've always known you were a practical man, Pez. You just have that look about you."

"Well, let me correct you. I don't believe in most superstitions, but I've had my moments."

"Like what? What spooked you?"

"Well… first, I should tell you that my father is from Argentina, and my mother is Chilean. When I was a child in Argentina, my parents used to tell stories to make me and my siblings behave. And one of the stories that scared me the most was the tale of the *El Pombero* and *El Familiar.*" El Pombero was this elusive, mysterious imp-like creature with large hands, large hairy feet, shaggy hair, and big eyes. He was also jet black."

"Sounds like the boogeyman."

"He is, and he was accompanied by this big headless, demonic, black dog, El Familiar, that wore a big chain around his neck that always dragged on the ground. Both were demons, Satan's henchmen. Anything that happened bad was attributed to El Pombero. Anything evil was said to bring the wrath of El Pombero on a person, and the chain of El Familiar can be heard, dragging, coming for you. I bought into that as a kid. I remember working the sugar cane fields, thinking I would hear something, and freaking myself out on several occasions."

"So, what was it that you thought you heard?"

"You know, a chain dragging."

"Jared and Tyler laughed. "But Pez, wouldn't you be harvesting in broad daylights? What was there to be afraid of?"

"Have you ever seen a sugar cane field? It's as wide and as long as a soccer field, and the plants grow to be 9 to 10 feet tall. Your imagination can run wild when you're a kid. But now, I know better."

"How old were you?"

"Hmmm, I would say from age 9 to 13."

"What else were you afraid of, no vampires or werewolves?" Jared asked, drawing a nervous stare from Tyler.

"A vampiro and a lycan. Hmmm, not as much as I was afraid of El Pombero and El Familiar. I guess it depends on the culture. A vampiro and a lycan weren't played up as much as the Spanish myths and legends. I didn't grow up hearing about them, but I'm aware they are popular in North America. I've watched the movies. They were very entertaining."

"Fair enough."

"But... I have a cousin who believes she is a vampiro. Her parents had to take her to one of those head doctors. She was loco, demente," Pez said, circling his finger while pointing to his head.

"Crazy?"

"Siii..."

"What happened to her?"

"She ran away... last I heard, she was living in the States."

"No shit? It figures. That's where all the vampires live," Jared laughed.

It was well into the evening, 7:45 pm to be exact, and the sun had finally set over the mountains. The trio had found a small cave, a grotto (Pez's term), and decided to spend the night. Jared was excited about his chance to finally "rough it" out in the open. The camping specialist back at the sporting store had made sure he and Tyler were well equipped for their maiden trekking expedition, plus he'd probably exploited them, selling them merchandise they didn't need. Regardless, Jared was eager to use his *SOL* thermal sleeping bag and tent. He had also brought water, a *Mountain House* 3-day meal kit, sun blocker, and a first-aid kit, same as Tyler. Jared was ready, for better or worse.

"Aaaa cho!" Tyler sneezed. "Sorry, something's in here, causing me to sneeze."

"No doubt. Maybe it's the draft. I'm snugged and tucked in. I kinda like this sleeping bag. How 'bout you, bro?"

"I'll be okay, until a snake crawls in here with me," Tyler cracked.

"Wha… what? There are snakes around here?"

Pez laughed. "He's just messing with you. Snakes aren't usually found at this altitude, plus it's not that much to eat around here."

"Good," Jared said, relieved. Tyler knew Jared was afraid of snakes.

"Let's try to get up around seven tomorrow. It's only

8:20 now. Say we shut it down around 9. That'll give us about 10 hours to sleep. Who needs that much sleep?"

"I do," Tyler said. I didn't sleep well last night. It's my chance to get some solid rest. Plus, after drinking those beers, along with the hiking and this altitude, I feel my body needs the rest."

"Well I'm not tired, I didn't drink as much as you two," Jared admitted. "But there's nothing else to do... in a cave with two knuckleheads – no offense, Pez."

"Si," Pez smiled, snacking on his candy. "If you want, I can tell you more about my land, more stories. It'll put you to sleep."

"Oh yeah? I would like that. Go for it. Whaddayou say, Tyler? ...Tyler?"

Tyler didn't respond. He had already begun to snore.

CHAPTER 11

April 6th started cool and breezy. The trio decided to ascend the mountain westwards, thereby circling the hill. It was hopefully the best way to cover as much ground possibly, while being ever alert, looking for a sign of a green flag, or any banner.

"Did you get enough sleep?"

"Yes, I feel like a new man. I think I'm going to start sleeping in caves more," Tyler joked. "How did you guys sleep?"

"Quite well, I didn't get remotely cold. I was encased like a cocoon in that sleeping bag. What time did you drift off, Pez? Last I remembered was you telling me about six stories – all starting with 'El'. There was El Cucuy, El Chupa..."

"I fell asleep around 12:15... and I recall telling you the tale of El Chupacabra," Pez said.

"Yeah, that one, and several others."

"Yes, I remember, which one did you like, if any?"

"I liked them all, but I was creeped out by the story of the man who killed his father and took his guts home to be cooked by the mother."

"Oh, you're talking about El Silbon."

"Yeah, that one… pretty gruesome stuff."

"Si, there are many, many tales and myths. Some with happy endings, most without. Some are silly, but all have a moral."

"I think it's the same in every culture."

The trek up the Ojos del Salado was surprisingly easy. So much so that Jared found it incredible that he and Tyler hadn't ever considered hiking as a physical outlet for exercising. They came across more nieves penitentes, even more closely grouped and spectacular than the ones seen earlier yesterday, as the brothers took the opportunity to pose for pictures under the vermilion sunrise. The air was cold and crisp, with a slight scent of sulfur.

"Aaaah, the mountain welcomes us. Today will be a good day," Jared pronounced.

Tyler, forever a cynic, rolled his eyes and looked at Jared with jest. "Why don't you ask the mountain to show us what we're searching for, while it's welcoming you."

"She will, my skeptical friend, you'll see," Jared said to his brother.

"I'm beginning to think this is an exercise in futility."

"Yeah, yeah, yeah. Ye of little faith."

"I have faith. I believe we will probably reach the peak

of this mug before coming across what we're looking for, if then."

"Why are you fucking whining?! Who wanted to come here? Bitch, bitch, bitch – that's all you ever do!" Jared said, fed up with Tyler's incessant bellyaching.

Tyler wisely didn't respond. He knew Jared was just trying to spin a positive vibe on everything, and he was grateful, but he was also frustrated - they both were. Both felt the pressure of staring at the possibility of being disappointed.

They continued hiking the mountain, albeit silently, with the brothers talking through Pez whenever they had something to say. The weather was a tolerable 43 degrees, but with the wind chill factor, it felt like it was freezing. Jared had the foresight to bring binoculars and peered through them. Nothing he saw, except more rocks and more mountains. A second look revealed something reflective, perhaps a mirror. He'd hoped it was related to what they were looking for, but he reasoned that it was more likely other mountaineers gathering their gear. He passed the binoculars to Pez.

"Tell me, what is that?"

Pez took a look, without answering right away.

"Is that a light or some kind of reflective metal?"

"I don't... wait, it's some type of energy force, fading in and out."

Tyler looked at Jared with heightened interest. Gone was the petty dissonance. He was dying to take the binoculars and see for himself. "May I?" He asked.

When he saw the light, ebbing and flowing, he knew his search was over. He emphatically shook his brother's hand and hugged him. "We did it, lil' bro! We did it!"

"You think that's it?"

"I know that's it... that's not a natural light. It's glowing slowly, faintly, but I can see it. What other explanation for that light?"

Jared thought for a minute. He had no explanation for the light. This had to be it; he wanted to believe that was the destination.

"How long do you think it will take to get up there from here?"

"Hmmm, that's about a 50 feet lateral elevation from here," Pez said, looking through the binoculars. "Maybe an hour and a half, give or take."

"Okay. That's our destination, Pez."

The trio acted accordingly.

Jared was a prisoner of nervous anticipation. His hands were sweating in the 44-degree weather, and he found breathing more challenging than ever. He'd imagined several different scenarios but never came to a conclusive ending for this occasion. Now here he was, moments away from what he believed to be his salvation. He was 100% convinced that this was the right place because the green flag that he saw in his dream was waving frantically in the Andes wind, near the cave's front entrance. It was an indicator that the cave was occupied to the few casual hikers that would've ventured this far. No doubt, fewer still would've cared enough to find out who the occupants were, so the brothers understood why this spot was chosen, or any mountainous region.

As they hesitantly entered the cave, they called out.

"Hello, hello, is anybody here?"

For minutes, they called out. Gone was the glow they had seen earlier. The men saw no evidence of belongings, no water, no tent equipment. There was no sign of human existence.

"Where is everybody?"

"They could be farther inside. Most caves are deeper than what they appear," Pez said. "So, who are you looking for again?"

"We don't know," Jared admitted while glancing at Tyler. Then, he thought better of it. "Pez, I think it's time we come completely clean with you. You deserve to know the truth. Tyler nodded, giving Jared the okay. "We think we're under some type of spell that has altered us."

Pez looked on puzzled, trying to follow what Jared was telling him. "Si amigo… a spell?"

"Yes," Jared said, whispering. "I can imagine how crazy I sound, but I'm telling you the truth. I'm a vampire, and my brother's a werewolf."

"Si," Pez said. Jared could sense Pez wasn't buying it, so he decided to stop, for fear of scaring him, and God knows they needed their guide to get back home. So he dropped the conversation.

They continued going deeper through the cave. Stalactites and stalagmites were encountered, as well as other forms of speleothems, and a small stream of flowing water.

"I don't know about this," said Tyler. "This is looking creepier and creepier... like the set from that *John Carter* movie."

"Scared much, bro?"

"Yes, and you should be too," Tyler said.

"I never said I wasn't. Where could this water be going? I haven't seen a source of water around here, since leaving Laguna Verde."

"There's a salt lake crater on the mountain's summit, plus melting snow could be the culprit, amigo."

"If that's the case, there must be an opening at the opposite end of the cave."

"You are probably correct. Do you want to keep pressing forward?"

Jared turned and looked at Tyler. "Well, what do you think?"

"We have come this far," he said, shrugging his shoulders. "...might as well go all the way."

"I agree. Pez, you heard the man, full speed ahead."

They followed the running stream to an opening. Everything was cold and pristine. Large and small boulders were strategically placed about, as though one had cleared the area, making a small salt pond the centerpiece.

"Well, somebody was out here not too long ago."

"So, where did they go?" Tyler asked.

"Maybe we're too late. Maybe we missed them."

It was strange hearing those words. Jared and Tyler never thought that getting here late, missing them, would ever be an issue. The forlorn emotion of disappointment hovered above them. Tyler, perhaps more than Jared, was particularly crestfallen. It was his wish, understandably, to lift the curse because of the transformation he goes through. The trio decided to rest there for a while. The emotional strain had zapped their energy. Pez, without fully understanding the situation, could see the brothers were disappointed, and in his way, tried to provide some solace.

"Here amigos… whenever I have a problem, I pop some of these and poof! All's better." Pez said, offering the brothers his candy.

Jared and Tyler were amused. Pez was right.

It was 1:45 in the afternoon. The trio had managed to eat and take a nap. The temperature had reached its high of 45 degrees, and all Jared and Tyler had to look forward to was another cold night in the Andes mountains. No way was that going to happen. So they began preparing the descent from the mountain, to return home.

"Pez, we are going to treat you to the best steak and lobster dinner in Santiago. You like steak and seafood, don't you?" Jared said.

"Oh si, siii, amigo. I can take you to the best restaurant in all of Santiago."

"Does this restaurant serve cold beer and alcohol?" said Tyler.

"Si, the very best, every restaurant serves alcohol."

"Great, so everybody's ready? You all packed, Tyler?"

"Yep."

"Has anyone seen my canteen, I left it with you?"

Jared never got a chance to answer. Before he could, the wind started gusting.

"What is it?!"

"I don't know, it looks like a storm," Pez said, guarding his eyes. Tyler suddenly turned, standing still, then instantly realizing, hoping, that this was the arrival of Abigail. He stood, with outstretched arms, like Christ the Redeemer, the famous statue in Rio. As the wind gusted and got more robust, it then gradually subsided until left in its wake were three human forms; astral, celestial, ethereal, dressed in robes. Tyler saw them as gods, and as one would expect, no introduction was needed. They knew who they were. But poor Pez, he was a frightening mess. He clenched his rosary beads and mumbled ¡Santa Madre de Jesús! ¡Santa Madre de Jesús! (Holy Mother of Jesus!)

After the wind diminished, only Abigail stepped forward, emitting a glowing luminescence. Her movement was slow and studied, but graceful as one would imagine a goddess would move. Just like in the dream, she spoke an ancient Anglo-Saxon language, but Jared and Tyler had no problem understanding her. Tyler kneeled to one leg, honoring her. Jared soon followed, but Pez stood frozen until Jared togged on the leg of his pants.

"Pez, kneel," Jared whispered.

Abigail motioned for the men to stand.

"Stand, I am not your queen. I'm Abigail, the men behind me are Ira and Elex."

"We know. We were hoping as much. It's our honored pleasure meeting you. Were you here all the while?"

"Aye. I wanted to study you first, observe your intentions. You are men on a purposeful course."

"Yes, we are. We were hoping that you could help us," Tyler said, timid and nervous.

"You are cursed, and you seek a cure, aye? I know. I summoned you and your brother, but the other, I feel no energy for him," Abigail said, referring to Pez.

"He's our guide, a friend."

"He fears me," Abigail said, observing Pez kneeling and praying.

"Forgive us. We have never seen one, such as yourself."

"Do not be afraid. Your eyes are beholding energy, for that's all we are."

"Energy," Tyler mumbled.

"Aye. Some energy goes to other places, but we were placed here never to leave the earth. As are you, so are we."

"So, is there any hope for us? Is there a cure?"

"Aye, my child, but only if you feel truly afflicted. There is a way to make you whole."

"There is? What must we do?"

"You must fight to conquer your fear, for your task is one of persistence and courage. Within a fortnight, one will try to use everything within her power to confuse and divide. The right will seem wrong, and wrong will seem right. To obtain what you are seeking, you will be risking what you already have. You will be risking your life."

"I understand. This one you speak of, are you referring to Asyla?"

"Aye, Asyla, she will use her powers to achieve her ultimate goal, which is to have everlasting life. Even now, her powers grow; with each awakening, she walks the earth longer, stronger, bringing about chaos, misery, and destruction wherever she goes. This is what she requires to obtain her goal," Abigail said, showing the men the Sacred Amulet worn around her neck. "With this, Asyla would walk the earth without needing to sleep. She would be eternally immortal, preeminent."

The men looked mesmerized, taking in all that Abigail had said. Her voice registered a pure placid tone that coated each syllable she annunciated. There was no need for a loudspeaker or megaphone. Her voice carried like a smooth rippleless current over an open wavelength.

"We must prevent her from ever possessing the Sacred Amulet. It would cause worldwide havoc, the likes of which you've never seen. We defeat Asyla. Then the order will be restored and halted until her next awakening. It is the single key to reversing the curse."

"After this awakening, when will you come back? When is the next awakening?"

"In the year 2357."

"Wow, I needn't worry. So I gather that you both awake together. So, do you sleep at the same time, all the time? Jared smiled while asking inquisitively.

"Asyla's awakenings always trigger when I awake, so aye, I am the guardian of the Sacred Amulet and humanity's best weapon against Asyla. It's the way of time and will forever be until she's completely destroyed."

"Wow, cool! Are there others like my brother and me?"

"Aye, there is, nine others to be precise. They were summoned too. So far, you are the only two that responded. Methinks my dreams were not recognized as summons. The new world is not vested in reading dreams. You have many other ways of communicating."

"Yes, we do. And yet, we are lost," Tyler said.

"Aye. Asyla will soon come for me. She has to. It's the only way to get what she so desires."

"So, why don't you stay hidden? Wouldn't your chances of not being found increase if you stayed asleep?"

"Aye, perhaps. But my chance to defeat her would also decrease. Though her greed for power propels her toward me, I should convey to you that I, like the wolf, am the predator, not Asyla. I need for her to find me."

Abigail was proud, strong, and quietly confident. No matter the task, she could instill courage into the worst of men. Tyler would follow her anywhere, so would Jared.

"So, what would you have us do?"

"Do you have suitable shelter?"

"Yes"

"Go there. Wait to hear from me. It shouldn't take long, for even now, I can feel her energy surging and getting stronger and stronger."

"You need but ask. We will be here."

Abigail, Ira, and Elex gradually disappeared into the blustery mountain air, just as they arrived.

CHAPTER 12

Jared and Tyler were trying to enjoy the charms of Santiago; they were trying. The fantastic ambiance and incredible food helped fulfill the brothers' promise they had made to Pez, sitting in the middle of the grand restaurant, *Aquí Esta Coco*. The girl flirting in the adjacent seat, with the devilishly incredible smile (she said her name was Angelica), made the meal that much more exquisite. All was as Pez said it would be, and more. But the memory of what had just transpired left the trio at a loss. Jared and Tyler were grateful to have come this far in their mission, but the reality of it all, the sheer actual idea of being there, witnessing and interacting, defied any pragmatism.

"Amigos... I cannot believe we lived through that. She let us go, after having seen her. Ya ya ya, no puedo creerlo, es simplemente increíble!"

Jared and Tyler laughed. "Why would you think that we were ever in danger?"

"Because she's a spirit, and most spirits are evil."

"And who told you that, Pez?"

"It's something my culture knows all too well. It's true."

"I thought you told me that you aren't superstitious?"

"I'm not, I'm practical, amigo… just stating facts."

"So I guess it's fair to ask, will you be our guide when we have to go back?"

Pez pondered for a minute. "You know, amigo… I'm not sure if I want to risk it again. I wish to be of help to you, but I might have to find another way. We have a saying in my country. It goes: Cuando el hacha pierde tu cuello, no te quedes para hacer preguntas.

"What does that mean?"

"It means, when the ax misses your neck, do not stand around to ask questions."

Jared laughed. "I like that… but surely you can't believe that your life was in any peril, do you?"

"Not so much then, but when you returned, maybe. The spirit lady said so herself."

"Yes, she did," Jared said solemnly while looking at Tyler. You have a point, but we must go. We can't achieve our mission without going."

"And what exactly is your mission?"

"Pez, I can't believe you are asking me that…we are here to reverse the curse… we are cursed, remember? You still doubt us, even after having witnessed Abigail?"

Pez thought for a minute. "I believe in Abigail... but you're asking me to believe in fairy tales. That's hard to comprender. Sorry, amigo."

Tyler placed his hand over Jared's. "Put yourself in Pez's shoes. Would you believe us? I don't think you would. And to be honest, I rather that he didn't. Nobody will ever believe him, and that's a plus for us."

"Maybe you're right... but I'm still a little perturbed that this little shit doesn't believe me," Jared smiled.

"Aaaah, but the wine is good and the cerveza's cold, amigo. Drink up!" Pez smiled.

Saturday, April 8th, presented a chance to explore the city. Jared and Tyler decided to rent bicycles and join a large crowd of locals, riding through Barrio Bellavista, an upscale, trendy neighborhood, boasting avant-garde galleries, hip restaurants, bars, and lordly mansions. The district laid between the Mapocho River and San Cristóbal Hill and was punctuated with tree-lined streets awash with colorful antique homes. As they rode, they were serenaded by the music's pulse coming from an array of clubs and disco bars. Many of the city's noted intellectuals and celebrities lived in the area, and on weekends like today, several art\craft markets run the length of the major vein along the river.

From Barrio Bellavista, they would visit Chile's National Zoo, located at the entrance of San Cristóbal Hill.

"Pretty cool, huh bro?"

"Yes, I'm digging it. This seems to be a cool place. I can see myself living here."

"You should... you have a great nightlife, great restaurants, good social activities, parks, museums, the currency exchange would be in your favor, and the women aren't half bad..."

"And what does that mean? Really, what the fuck does that mean?" Jared said.

"Just what I said... the women aren't that bad looking."

"Tyler, that's like saying they aren't that pretty. You're not committing to a yes or a no. I think the women are gorgeous, for goodness sake!"

"I like them. I do, but there are just a lot of little Indians running around here."

"And... so what? Not all are short. Half of Chile's population are Amerindians and Spanish. They're small people, that's to be expected. But the other half is very diverse, just like North America."

"I guess... I just prefer taller women."

"You're prejudiced."

"No, I have my biases, as do you."

Jared looked at Tyler as if he smelled, which provoked Tyler to say, "Lil' bro, we were raised by the same people, the same way - don't dare try to judge me. You know me better than anybody. You know I'm not prejudiced."

"Okay, if you say so, dude."

The brothers were coming upon a timely gathering and pulled off the road to see what the commotion was. It was a beer-stand, selling popular local and international craft beers and home-made meat pies.

"Let's have a look-see. I hadn't had a good meat pie since the New England State Fair last year," Jared said.

"*Quepazie's* back home has the best I've eaten."

"I'm not a big fan of theirs, too much sage or something. The spices they use are overbearing."

"That's exactly why I like their meat pies. I love the spices."

"Okay...I'm not going to fight you over them. You say tomatoes, I say tamatoes"

"Wow, that'll be something new. It seems we are always at each other's throats of late."

Jared thought pensively about what Tyler had said. He was right. They had been fighting a lot. "Bro, no matter what, you know I love you... I just wanted to tell you that."

"I love you too, Lil bro, no matter what... so let's try some of those meat pies."

The brothers ordered two meat pies, each, and two local IPA's. The meat pies were quite delicious, actually, and less spicy than the ones served at Quepazie's. They both liked them. After eating and making a few friends, they continued along the festive road to San Cristóbal Hill.

The San Cristóbal Hill (Cerro San Cristóbal) was

precisely that, a hill. The area elevated about 300 feet above the rest of the city, and one could take a funicular between different landscaped sections of the hill and catch a magnificent view of the town. At the summit was a white 72-foot statue of the Blessed Virgin Mary, which also had a small chapel within the pedestal. The Santiago Metropolitan Park rested at the base of the hill, next to the Chilean National Zoo. A later visit to the museum would follow.

It was a great outing, a successful outing. The brothers had garnered newfound respect for this exciting, resourceful city. It was now Monday, April 10th, two days removed since coming face to face with Abigail. There was little else to do except explore more of the city, but a new moon would be approaching tomorrow, a full moon. And as far as Tyler was concerned, one more transformation was one more too many.

"Question," Jared said while drinking his blood concoction. "What exactly is a fortnight?"

"Twelve days, I think… or is it 14 days?" Tyler replied.

"You're not sure?"

"Look it up, but I think it's 14 days."

"It is," Jared said, looking it up on his phone, "So we're going to have to wait two weeks?"

"Maybe… besides, Abigail said within a fortnight. It could be two days from now or next week unless you have something more important to do."

"No, of course not… was just thinking – there's a full moon coming up, isn't there?"

"Yes, tomorrow."

"What are you gonna do?"

"I'm hoping Abigail will contact us by then. If not, I'll probably get dropped off at the mountains somewhere. I figure I can't hurt anyone up there."

"What about the other hikers? There's bound to be someone hiking."

Tyler didn't answer immediately. He couldn't think of a suitable place where there would be no people. It was doing these times he sincerely wanted to die.

"Look… I'm doing the best I can, bro.

Can you think of a place I should go?"

"No brother, I can't… and I know you are doing your best. I think that going to the mountains is the appropriate thing to do; it's the most responsible thing, especially considering being this far from home."

"Then it's settled, I'm going… maybe I'll get lucky and see Abigail, who knows? Maybe she can help me out."

"Yeah… maybe. Do you want me to come along?" Jared said. He didn't want to come. He feared Tyler's transformation, but it was something that a brother should ask.

"Oh, I'm sure… no thanks, lil' bro. It'll be one less worry for me, but thanks."

"You want to go out and get a beer with me? Heard they have a fantastic microbrewery about 3/4th of a mile away. It'll be on me," Jared said, trying to alleviate his brother's troubled mind.

"No... no, I better not. We had a few beers yesterday. I'm still recovering."

"Are you sure? That didn't seem like a sure-fire definite. I hate drinking alone. I read here that they have some fantastic lagers, porters and IPA's... says here that there are hundreds of crafted and rare beers from all over the world."

"Does sound good, doesn't it? Do they serve food?"

"Yes, they say the finest."

Tyler thought for all of thirty seconds, then said: "okay, you've talked me into it, when are we leaving?"

"Now."

April 11th was a sunny brisk Chilean day, with all the hopeful promises that such a day should bring. The last time the brothers had seen Pez, it was quite profitable for the tour guide pilot. He received a thousand dollar tip, which was equivalent to 619,201 Chilean pesos, a small fortune. So despite what he had told them about having reservations about being their pilot during further excursions, well, let's just say that money talks; bullshit walks. It didn't take a lot of twisting of the arm, but to his relief, he didn't have to stay with Tyler, all he had to do was drop him off and come back for him later, which Pez found rather odd, but he didn't question. However, he did tease Tyler about having a secret rendezvous with Abigail.

"Senor Tyler, the mountains hold many, many secrets.

A man can reinvent himself, for better or worse. It's no problem, amigo. The spirit lady was beautiful."

"Yeah, Tyler, we understand why you don't like pretty Chilean women now. " Jared teased, from the back seat. "They don't have that certain supernatural quality to them... that certain 'je ne sais quoi'," Jared said, joining Pez in teasing Tyler.

"Ha. Ha. You guys got jokes. I wish. Just be back here around noon tomorrow.

"Noon? We got you. Okay, you got food, your gear, matches, a flashlight, your phone, even though it doesn't work up here. Can you think of anything else you would need?"

"Naw bro, I'm set. Just have me a girl and a cold beer waiting for me when I get back."

"A Chilean girl? But you don't like those," Jared laughed.

Tyler smiled. Jared was genuinely concerned for Tyler's well-being but remained upbeat in his presence.

Pez was able to find a clearing on the mountains to land the helicopter, which made it much easier since their last visit.

"So Pez, why weren't you able to land the 'copter' in the mountains the first time we were here?" Jared asked.

"Because you didn't know where you were going. I didn't know if your destination was the first part of the mountain, the middle, or near the top, ¿entender? So it was best to start as we did."

"I guess he told you!" Tyler laughed.

"Yeah, he did... but hey, bro, take good care of yourself. If you can, meet us back at this spot by noon tomorrow, alright? Jared said, hugging his brother tightly while screaming over the rotary blades of the helicopter. Tyler shook Pez's hand and gradually stepped backward. A final wave and he was on his way.

Jared and Pez watched until he disappeared in a hollowed cráter in the mountain.

"Don't worry, he'll be okay, amigo," Pez assured Jared. "Is he going to see the spirit woman?"

"Let's hope so. I would feel better if that occurred."

"Of course, he will. Why else would he come up here alone?"

"I wouldn't know, Pez. I wouldn't know."

That night, Jared dreamt. He saw Tyler in his dream in mid-transformation; half-human, half-werewolf - shirtless. He was kneeling in front of a tall woman facing him, but her back was toward Jared. It wasn't Abigail, because her hair was dark and she had an olive complexion. Abigail was fair, with blonde hair. There was a ceremony of some sort performed, Jared couldn't tell if Tyler was being inducted or sacrificed. There was a servant (slave) by the tall lady's side, holding a big scythe. Jared reasoned that Tyler was drugged. He was too passive and docile, following orders subserviently. He was given a drink from a golden goblet. Then he handed it back to the servant. Without hesitation, the servant made one sure swoosh of the scythe, severing Tyler's head from his body, the body tumbled forward like a bucket of water.

Jared woke up in a cold sweat. He sat still on the bed for minutes, heaving heavily, refusing to believe the dream. It's but a vision, he told himself. Not all of his dreams are significant manifestations of truth. He used to dream all the time, and that was all this was; merely a dream. He found himself crying. It means nothing. "Nothing!" he voiced out loud.

The time was 4:22 a.m., and Jared couldn't sleep. He got out of bed immediately. Everything was a blur. He had to get in touch with Pez, but was afraid to call. He couldn't think of anybody else to lean on, but he needed help. He had to call, then he thought, the helicopter company where Pez worked wouldn't be open until 8:00. It would be useless calling him before then. He decided to wait.

Waiting 4 hours under such circumstances is excruciating. It's pure hell. Jared managed to get ahold of Pez, and surprisingly he was already awake. Jared told Pez that Tyler was in trouble, maybe worse, and would explain in detail what was going on once they were en-route.

En-route, Jared did his best to explain.

"Amigo, remember the spirit lady said that the other lady would try to confuse you; that right would seem wrong, up would seem down... I think it was an illusion, amigo. I think your brother is alive."

"You really think so, Pez?"

"Si. Si, amigo. I think your brother is fine."

"God... I pray you are right. I have no plan, except going to the same cave where we saw Abigail. You don't have to come, just drop me off where you landed yesterday."

"Si... but I will come if you want me to."

"You will? I appreciate that."

"No problem, amigo."

CHAPTER 13

April 12th, it was 10:47 a.m. when Jared and Pez reached Abigail's cavern. The cold dark dwelling offered crude shelter, but Jared was grateful for the shade. He was getting more and more at ease with the nocturnal aspect of, well, everything because the glare from the snow and sun was becoming unbearable. Jared didn't wait to get halfway through the cave before making his announcement.

"Hello... Hello, Abigail!" He called out, waiting moments before calling again. "Hello, I need to talk with you... please! Jared waited, nervously chatting with Pez.

"I'm not sure how all of this works," He admitted to Pez.

"Si, she's probably on lunch break," Pez managed to chuckle.

"Yeah," Jared smiled. "She's gotta be here. What time do you have?"

"It's 11:16, still early."

"I'm going to wait. I don't have anything better to do. Maybe Abigail's busy with her spiritual chores."

"Si."

Jared and Pez walked through the cave, past the speleothems, to the clearing in the cave. Abigail appeared here first. Maybe she'll be comfortable enough to show herself again, Jared thought. So he tried calling.

"Hello! Abigail, hellooooo! Jared Jace here. I need to speak to you. I need to see you, please!"

Jared had only to wait three minutes before a gush of wind appeared, then the fog. When the mist dissipated, three figures came into sight, with Abigail, Ira, and Elex looking supremely celestial in their godlike aura, with the same glowing luminescence.

"My lady, forgive me for the disturbance, but I need your help."

"Aye."

"My brother... I received an image in a dream," Jared said, starting to sob. "I saw him slain, beheaded early this morning, he's dead."

"Take heart, my son. I feel your brother's energy. He is not dead, but he's in great peril."

"He's not... he's not dead?"

"Nay, he's very much alive, for now."

"But I dreamt the image, I saw him. It seemed so real."

"You saw what Asyla wanted you to see. Remember, she's a conjurer, a seer, and an enchantress. She has many wiles at her disposal. The dream was trick, used to influence you into coming to look for him."

"But why would she do that?"

"For your blood… your souls. Asyla is more your ancient mother than me. The blood of a vampire and a lycan mix is second only to the Sacred Amulet's power. With you and your brother in her covenant, it may well tilt the power balance closer. She aims not to destroy you, at least not right away, but to use you for your blood. The goal for every creature of the night is to walk the earth during daylight. That feat can be accomplished with you and your brother's blood."

"Why didn't you warn me… why wasn't my brother warned that Asyla was nearby?"

"You and your brother were warned as soon as I knew. I contacted both of you last evening. You didn't receive it because you were awakened by Asyla's dream. I can't communicate from a distance unless you are asleep."

Jared knew Abigail was correct because he couldn't go back to sleep last night.

"Your brother had to have been captured by Asyla during the last evening. His vibe is strong. I sense he is angry and confused, but his heart beats sturdy. He is alive."

"Thank God," Jared said. He gazed over at Pez, looking just as awe-stricken and mystified as the first time he saw Abigail. "So what must I do, how can I help my brother?"

"It's best that you stay here, or risk capture. You have food and robes?"

"Yes," Jared said.

"Then you should find all that you need here," Abigail said, without catering to the sensibilities of modern man. In the world from which she hailed, one appreciated the concept of basic amenities, no questions asked.

"Asyla will come to us soon, and your brother will be with her. It won't be long. I will be here when you need me." With that said, she, Ira, and Elex gradually faded."

"Wow, that is so cool, amigo! I don't think I will ever get tired of seeing that," Pez said.

"So now, you are cool with Abigail?"

"I don't see her as a threat any more if that's what you mean. One day, I'm going to figure out how she's doing all of this."

Jared laughed. "When you do, let me know."

"So what are we going to do the rest of the day in a cave, amigo? Are you seriously going to stay here?"

"I think I have to, you heard her."

"But amigo, It's only noon, and we're not that far from the helicopter. We can go back to town and come back whenever she contacts you."

"No Pez, it doesn't work that way. I can't leave Tyler. You can go back, but I seriously hope you won't."

"Don't worry, amigo. I'll come back for you."

"That's not what I'm worried about," Jared said, looking Pez dead into his eyes. "Look, I'm worried about your health. This isn't a game, Pez. Do you understand what I'm saying to you? There's a blood-thirsty, evil bitch out there. We are fortunate to have made it to the cave. You are taking a risk going back to the helicopter."

"It's broad daylight, and the 'copter is less than a mile away, maybe closer than that. What could possibly happen to me? I just can't stay in this cave all day, amigo. I can't. I would go stir crazy. Besides, I forgot to tell you; I have another client today."

"Okay, Pez, okay. I wish you would stay. There's evil all around us. Abigail wasn't lying."

Pez reached in his backpack and showed Jared a .45 caliber Sig Sauer pistol. "You see this? This baby is all the protection I need. Don't worry about me, amigo. I'll be just fine."

Jared looked on with tears in his eyes. Fearing this would be the last time he would see his buddy, he hugged Pez tightly.

"Well, I guess there's nothing I can say to make you change your mind. Take good care, my friend."

"You will see me again, amigo. I promise."

Jared smiled and patted Pez's on his shoulder without saying a word.

"I'll be back. You will see," were Pez's last words before leaving the cave.

8:40 p.m. Jared was awakened by what he perceived as water, cave drippings from melted snow, but to his horror, the droplets were red! Blood! Blood drops on a man's face can drive him crazy and make him jump out of his skin, especially if it's a constant drip, as warm as it was coursing through an unfortunate victim's body. At first, Jared feared the worst, but the corpse suspended over him was not Pez's or his brother, but rather another unfortunate mountaineer. The body was drained of all bodily fluids, as it was just another mind-game trick played by Asyla. She had put two of her mindless henchmen up to the task. Jared was now beginning to understand the insidious nature of this she-devil. People were but a pawn to her; to be used and discarded however she saw fit. They didn't mean a thing to her, and her ultimate turn-on was to break down her target mentally. Jared, for better or worse, was now singled out as a target, as Tyler had been captured.

After disposal of the body, Jared turned his thoughts to other things. Pez must have made it to safety. That was good. He could now have a single-minded focus on rescuing Tyler. He had no perception of how that feat would occur, but he trusted that he would get that opportunity at some stage.

IT STARTED WITH SICK, wretched laughter and the cave bats, disturbed, flying about haphazardly. It went on for minutes, the insidious, woebegone laughter, shrieking incessantly and loudly. Jared looked around, but there was no one in sight. "Abigail!" He called out loud but wasn't sure she could hear him over the commotion. But like a good neighbor, Abigail appeared, arriving in her customary gust of wind, with Ira and Elex in a defensive stance.

Yet the maniacal laughter continued, with the shrieking and screaming. It was a chaotic tactic to confuse. Asyla seemed everywhere, but Abigail stood her ground, poise and levitating slightly above the ground, ready to counter-attack anything Asyla might throw at her. She knew Asyla wouldn't be at full strength until midnight and sometimes there afterward. So her deploying this tactic was unusual for her. But then, she was dealing with an unpredictable deviation of all that's normal.

Suddenly, the shrieking screams stopped, followed by silence. Jared moved closer to Abigail. For minutes no sound was heard; just eerie silence, too bizarre for comfort, but then a fluttering sound could be heard getting louder and louder, closer and closer.

"Take cover. It's bats!" Jared hollered, running to hide behind the nearest rock and stalagmite formation. Thousands of bats flew through the cave, practically occupying the entire space of the cavity. The bombardment lasted for three minutes, followed by spectral apparitions of macabre deaths. There were images of beheadings, earthquakes, homicides, airplane crashes, massacres, drownings, suicides, and people dying in wars. All of which she must've had a part in orchestrating. All of which would've made a timid person stop in their tracks and reconsider.

Then finally, she appeared; statuesque, stately, and majestically evil. Her long dark mane seemed to be alive, and like Abigail, she could levitate and hover. But what was inexplicably noticeable about Asyla, was that she had a long forked tongue, like a serpent. She spoke slowly and deliberately, hauntingly, and cold.

"Abigail... finally, we meet again, my old adversary."

"Aye."

"... and I see you bothered to bring your trusted companions.

"Aye, as always."

Asyla gazed over at Jared, but he didn't warrant mentioning. After all, he was just a weakling human, mere food, only there for her amusement.

"I ask, sister, once again, will you return the Sacred Amulet to its rightful owner?"

"Once again, the answer is nay. The amulet is with its rightful owner."

"Liar! You and your family have stolen from my family for years! My family owned the cave where you found the amulet. Therefore everything that came out of that cave was owned by the Malucos."

"Nobody owned that land. Even so, the answer is still nay."

Asyla grazed upon Abigail with pure disdain for several seconds, then she spoke, tongue darting in and out of her mouth. "You claim that you care for these humans. You speak of a divine cause when these maggots kill and mutilate each other. You've sacrificed, healed, and saved, only to walk away without any gratitude shown your way. When will you learn that these pests are nothing more than nuisances?" She said, her disdain ever-present. "They have made the same mistakes over and over, for centuries. They're incapable of learning, and if I don't wipe millions away at a time, the world would have surely been overrun with them, and collapsed...they are roaches! My sister, I plea to you, let us rule together. Let us take our rightful throne, side by side, like the true queens we are," Asyla said, holding out her hand. "We have walked this earth longer than they can dare fathom. We were destined to rule. Come, my sister. It's time to fulfill our destiny together."

Abigail didn't blink, nor was she moved by Asyla's offer. "And how should we rule, my sister - by kindly benevolence, or ruthless evil? When would you put a stalk in my heart, be it ten years? A hundred years? Ten thousand years from now?" Abigail said.

"Why I would never... "

"You would never be more than a selfish, self-serving murderer. Your treachery knows no bounds. You destroyed our villages; you slaughtered my people, your people - your own parents. You should have never been born; nature made a mistake - a cruel, horrible mistake."

"Be still your tongue, witch! Have you so easily forgotten what I'm capable of?" Asyla said as she was getting angry.

But Abigail continued. "You are sick, Asyla, ill... have been since your very existence. You should have been treated for your malady eons ago. The world would have been spared your cruelty and your mindless chaos, but I have something to offer you."

Asyla breathed heavily, incensed by Abigail's words. "What do you have to offer me?" She asked.

"Some advice… go back to sleep. Sleep long and hard, and you might avoid destruction. You are a sick abomination. Begone, Asyla! Be gone."

Asyla began to laugh in her sick, incessant way. Then, without warning, her tongue rapidly darting in and out of her mouth, she hurled what appeared to be a lightning bolt in Abigail's direction, barely missing her and hitting the wall of the cave. The bolt was accompanied by a clash of sparks and lightning that boomed and thunder-clapped, crackling the air with an explosive expansion of fire that appeared to hit Asyla. But Asyla wasn't hit. Five of her minions rushed in, carrying a shirtless man on a stake. It was a lethargic Tyler. They posted him between Asyla and Abigail's strike zone, knowing that Abigail would be reluctant to return fire for fear of hitting him. But Elex and Ira covered the flanks from the side, savagely attacking her minions, ripping throats and slinging their bodies against the cave's wall.

Upon seeing Tyler, Jared called out for him, but Tyler didn't respond.

"Abigail! Abigail, you want this human? He's going to die soon without help. You know it, we both know it. Give me his brother, and you can have him, get him some help," she laughed, fiendishly, then fired another lightning bolt in Abigail's direction, hitting some stalagmites.

Abigail conjured up a hailstorm and sent it flying back towards Asyla while managing to avoid Tyler. The hail projectiles toppled many of her minions, with a couple scurrying for shelter. Not to be bested, Asyla sent a hurricane flying at Abigail. Jared laid in a fetal position behind the rock formation. It was all he could do to keep from getting pulverized from the flying debris. Abigail then countered with more lightning bolts, while continuing her assault of hailstorms. So violent was her retort, rocks and boulders were split in half.

The entire cave lit up from all the electricity! The two titans went at it for twelve solid minutes, without either giving ground. It wasn't until Elex and Ira's annihilation of Asyla's underlings did the tide seemed to tilt in Abigail's favor, and yet Asyla refused to give in. Asyla had gotten stronger since they last fought, and she didn't mind displaying her full strength. With a clink of her wrist braces, she summoned a blizzard. The snowfall was so heavy that visibility was minimal. Abigail couldn't see her target, so she waited and maneuvered three feet to her left. If she couldn't see Asyla, Asyla surely shouldn't be able to see her. As soon as she had a hint of visibility, she signaled Elex and Ira, who was once again flanking her, to attack at the same time. They responded by sending waves of broken stalactites and stalagmites, accompanied by lightning at Asyla. It was enough to trip her, but not before she grabbed Tyler, using him as a shield. Abigail could tell by Tyler's flaccidity that he was void of life. He had probably been dead before they brought him in.

Abigail conjured up an avalanche of rocks and boulders, toppling Asyla immediately. Asyla tried to recover, but before she could, Abigail sent a lightning bolt, striking her in the chest. Asyla howled, letting out a monstrously piercing cry, as she laid mortally wounded. Abigail moved closer, removing a jagged knife affixed to the belt on her side. Without ceremony, she struck Asyla in her chest, brutally ripping out her heart. With Asyla's heart in one hand and the Sacred Amulet in the other, Abigail held them both high above her head, reciting an ancient spell. "Echa tu mael caemino en el biylogng eray, yo te envío a bact demonios… Echa tu mael caemino en el biylogng eray, yo te envío a bact demonios…" The spell was repeated five total times, with Elex and Ira joining her. Suddenly the Sacred Amulet glowed, emitting a laser-like beam in the area where Asyla had fallen, opening the earth and swallowing her minions. Elex and Ira then rolled Asyla's body into the ground cavity.

Jared finally raised his head to see snow, smoke, and ash, but not his brother. He frantically searched for Tyler and saw one limp arm sticking out from the devastation.

"Tyler! Tyler!" He called out, scrambling through the rubbish to reach him. "Oh, Tyler… no, no, noooo. God, please, no," he cried, trying to shake Tyler's lifeless remains into responding. Tyler, wake up, oh god noooo," he continued to sob, holding his brother. "This wasn't supposed to happen, not like this, not like this."

Abigail and Ira gathered around him. They had seen

this scenario much too often, yet they couldn't bring any solace to Jared.

"We are sorry for your loss, Jared Jace, he died honorably."

"No, he was nothing more than a mere sacrifice," Jared said distraughtly. "We never asked for this. He didn't deserve this."

"He gave up his life for you. Asyla couldn't have drunk of his blood unless he allowed it. Asyla used him, hoping to get next to you, but he gave up his life to save yours. We call that honor. You are released from your curse, Jared Jace."

"Released? How do you know?"

"Your thirst for blood is gone, is it not?"

Jared touched his throat. "I… I don't know. I can't tell. I have no hunger or thirst for anything right now."

"Understandable. We will stand on this plane of existence for three moons. After that, we won't appear again until Asyla awakes."

"You mean, she's not dead?! After all of that, she still lives? You ripped out her goddamn heart, for god sakes!"

"Aye, there's a possibility she still lives. Her body was destroyed, but not her soul-energy, not completely. I still feel her energy - very faint, but still there, nonetheless."

"I hate that the bitch wasn't destroyed! Something about this doesn't seem fair. I've lost my brother, but she still lives. She should be dead!"

"You have the right to be angry. You have that right.

But fear not, you will never have to deal with Asyla again in your lifetime."

"I know I sound bitter and ungrateful," he said, not bothering to look up. Then he gathered his composure the best he could. "Look, I want you to know that I'm grateful for all you have done and sacrificed. I'm just a little angry, but I'll be okay. Again, I thank each of you very, very much."

"Fair well, Jared Jace." And just like that, the trio slowly disappeared into the fog. Jared felt exhausted, but he would clean Tyler's body before getting rest. Tyler never liked being cold, so he washed his torso with a washcloth and placed one of his shirts on him. It was 12:45 a.m. Jared prepared his sleeping bag precisely as Tyler would have done, and propped Tyler's body next to him. He would read, cry, and reminisce with Tyler. Then after that, he would fall asleep next to his brother one final time.

To Jared's surprise, Pez survived, and everything was as he'd said: He didn't get harmed, and he showed up, as promised - which was a great relief for Jared. He wondered how he would get Tyler's body off the mountain, but trusty ole Pez made that a non-issue. God bless Pez.

When Jared relayed what had happened, he was just as sad and distraught over Tyler. They were genuine friends, despite the brevity of knowing one another, and Pez swore never to forget Tyler.

"I hope you can forgive me. I should've been here for you, but I was afraid. I was a coward. I'm sorry, amigo."

"No need to apologize. You have been a big help to me, and Tyler too."

"If you like, we can take care of funeral arrangements here in Santiago. We can have the ceremony done quickly, which is our custom. It's up to you, amigo."

"No… no, but thanks… I think I will have him flown back home."

"I was hoping you would stay around a little longer, but I understand."

"This won't be the last you'll see of me. I'll be back."

"I hope so, amigo… but first, we will have to contact the park police. They have to do an investigation of all deaths that happen in the mountains. What will you tell them?"

Jared hadn't thought about the investigation. In fact, he hadn't thought of any legalities concerning Tyler's death, which reminded him, there was another body to account for in the cave. How would he explain the deaths without arousing suspicion? "I honestly don't know. Who would believe me if I told them the truth? Nobody," he said, answering his own question. What should I tell them?"

"How did Tyler die, I mean, what did he die from?"

"I don't know… I couldn't tell you if it was tortured from Asyla or if he died from one of their exchanges. I've never seen anything like that. It's hard to explain."

"From the looks of things, I would say three bombs were set off. You can tell them that. I would believe that explanation."

"And how would you explain the bodies' lack of blood?"

"Huh?"

"…both bodies were drained of blood, were you listening to me?"

"Yes, amigo, I missed that part. Maybe they won't ask."

"Oh yeah… hey, give me a hand with this, will you?" Jared said while attempting to zip Tyler into his sleeping bag. "Bye, brother, you didn't deserve this." He kissed Tyler's forehead.

"We should move the other body to a different part of the cave, that way, the two deaths won't look connected if ever found," Pez said. Jared agreed, so the other body was moved further to the back of the cave, underneath some rocks.

Later, they proceeded to carry Tyler's body over the short distance to where Pez had landed the helicopter. Jared would have to get his story together then. He was just too tired to think at the moment.

The next day, the park police and investigators ruled Tyler's death as "accidental cave-in," meaning the cave imploded. His body revealed several compound fractures due to the cave collapsing, authorities believed. The lack of blood in his system was explained as having severe acute anemia, probably due to the high altitude. However, there was one highly suspicious investigator, but he was in no possession of scientific evidence, so he was ignored. All that was left was for Jared to arrange a way home.

On Saturday, April 15th, Jared said goodbye to Pez and the city of Santiago.

"I plan on living a part of my life in this city one day," he told Pez. "I love it here."

"When that day comes, Santiago would welcome you with open arms, amigo!"

"Huh, I almost forgot. Here's a little going away present from Tyler and me," Jared said, handing Pez an envelope containing a certified check. When Pez opened the envelope and looked inside, he cried. The check was for $50,000.

"So long, my friend."

"Adiós, mi amigo," Pez said between tears.

The two friends hugged, and Jared was on his way.

Watson took Tyler's death hard, perhaps harder than Jared would've imagined, considering he, himself, was thought to be Watson's favorite of the two brothers. But then, Watson never voiced those words. It was Jared's private opinion simply because he cared for Watson more. After Tyler's funeral, Watson took off three weeks to mourn.

Jared gave up his expensive condominium and moved into Tyler's house. He'd always liked the house, so he entirely decorated it and added a fence, which emphasized the roving three and a half acreage it rested on. There would be other improvements too, like a huge pool and a tennis court, but first, he designed a full room that was a shrine to Tyler.

On the business front, a statue of Tyler and himself was designed and placed near the building's front entrance. Watson had the company positioned to show its highest yields ever! The stock was trending through the roof. Because of recent developments, the board acknowledged Jared's acquisition of Tyler's shares, making him the unquestionable, undisputed owner and CEO of the company, a title he had no trouble relinquishing to Watson. For the first time in a long while, Jared was able to relax and enjoy drinking a bottle of wine without mixing it with blood. He'd never believed he was a full-fledged vampire, but he was well on his way to becoming one. Now that he had been tested and medically cleared of any ailment, he felt he had a new lease on life.

Life couldn't get any better, or could it?

Later that summer, he met a pretty, but shy, pre-med student, named Claire Hanley while at the job on a construction site. With two dates under his belt and a third date promised, things were looking good. He next enrolled in an aviation class. He saw the newfound freedom that flying could afford him, and was very serious when he told Pez and Tyler that he wanted to give it a try. He would do it for Tyler.

It was now Friday, April 28th. Jared had promised Claire that they would take in a play after dinner. He came home early to get a head start on the evening. He poured himself a glass of wine, sat on his couch, and took it all in. Life had its occasional disappointments, but it had its up times too. He was one of the fortunate ones. He was blessed, and he knew it. He had pledged to live for himself and Tyler – try to enjoy doubly as much, and be grateful for all of life's excesses.

He laid across his bed, eventually falling asleep. He slept for almost three hours until an abrupt noise awakened him. He stirred and turned, finally getting up to go downstairs, drowsy and lethargic. As he entered the kitchen and was about to open the refrigerator, a shadow flashed by him. He left the refrigerator door open and walked to the living room. Startled, he saw a lady sitting on his sofa with a drink in her hand. At first, he thought it was one of Tyler's friends that he had given a key to the door. He moved closer, wiping his eyes to get a better view.

"Hello... hello, if you're here for Tyler, he isn't in," he said, looking over the lady's shoulder. "I'm afraid I have some bad..." He stopped in his tracks.

What he saw shook his consciousness into a state of shock! He checked again, pinching his arm, to make sure he was fully awake. He was. There, on his sofa, sat Nayla Lloyd in the flesh!

Jared's heart started palpitating so hard, he felt the thumping in his chest, for he knew why she was here. He stood, frozen, daring not to say a word. He had never been so afraid – not even in the middle of Abigail and Asyla's battle. He dared not talk. He dared not breathed.

"Hello Jared, imagine seeing me here," she said, witty as ever. Jared didn't respond. He was too scared.

"Ayy now, the cat's got your tongue? You weren't this quiet the last time we were together. In fact, you charmed the dress right off of me." She snickered wickedly.

A chill ran down his spine. He didn't know what to say or do.

Nayla stood, looking around. "My, you've done a great job with this place since last I was here, haven't you? You know, I've been coming here, waiting for you. I missed you on two other occasions and thought you had moved on, but persistence pays off."

"Nayla… I know I've done wrong by you, but it wasn't me. I was under a curse. I was sick, not of any fault of my own. I'm not that man anymore, nor am I a slave to the curse. I'm completely human now, just a man. Look, I can give you anything. Anything you want in this world, you need but ask. I'm worth over 440 million dollars. You can ha… "

"Shhhhh," she said, pressing two fingers to his lips. It was as though Jared's words never registered with her. "I don't want your money, Mr. Jace… you left me wrapped on a cold tarp. Imagine waking up, not knowing where you are, cold, hungry, alone. I remember lying there, not knowing if I was dead or alive, not knowing what you had done to me until later that night. I never went back home because I can't trust myself around those I love, so I sit and watch my family go about their nightly activities from a distance. I'm alone. I no longer have a family." She said, then turned, looking Jared dead in his eyes. "I hunger, Jared… it's insatiable. I'm always hungry – not for food, can you imagine? Can you imagine never feeling satisfied, can you, Jared? This life… this nightmare is a lonely hell; I've killed people, Jared - innocent people - four to be precise! I've got to live with that, if you call this living," She said, with eyes welling up with tears. "You say you can give me anything in the world that I want?"

"Yes, I can. I swear it. Anything that money can buy, just request it."

"Can you give me back my old life?"

Jared looked on hopelessly without saying a word.

"Can you give me back my family? That's what I want the most. It's all that I've ever wanted… can you? Can you?!" She screamed. "Because I don't give a damn about your money, your millions!"

"I'm sorry, Nayla. I'm so, so sorry," Jared responded, tears running down his face.

"I loved you, Jared… I know we didn't have long, but I loved you."

"Jared didn't respond. He knew there were no words to justify what he had taken away from Nayla. A walk to his veranda was accompanied by Nayla, silently following him. Smiling through his tears, he said, "You know…the irony in this life we share is neither of us asked for it, but we both shall pay a heavy price. I never gave much credence to the thing about the cross, never thought much about garlic, and that saying about a vampire not being able to see himself in a mirror – that's a bunch of crock! I didn't think twice about it, because I knew it was pure Hollywood. But the one thing I should've been wary of was a vampire's victim coming back from the dead…" He said, shaking his head.

"You should've burned me to ashes, baby. You would've done both of us a favor," Nayla said, stepping closer. "It's time, Jared… are you ready?"

Jared took a final gaze of the magnificent Maine skyline. He had always admired the subtle green, red, and blue of the northern aurora. "Yes… yes, I'm ready. It's a beautiful night to die."

Nayla moved closer, caressing his hair until she had had a handful, exposing his neck. Her two-inch long incisors punctured his jugular vein, draining the sweet essence from his body, voiding him of life, itself.

She let out a bloodcurdling guttural scream and cried, mightily. It was over.

~ FINI ~

Zoe Jackson is a photographer, poet, writer, and author of *The Bianchi Files*. *Dhampir, The Blood Curse* is his second novel. A native of Shreveport, Louisiana, he now resides in Atlanta, Georgia. You can connect with Zoe at

www.facebook.com/zoe.jackson.3551

and

www.instagram.com/zoe.jackson.3551

www.ingramcontent.com/pod-product-compliance
Lightning Source LLC
Chambersburg PA
CBHW031139130726